'I haven't go

'Of course you ha

'You don't know

'But I know a great deal about you. You have typical Sagittarian flair and warmth, the ability to act, to play the clown, perhaps to hide a more serious side, the willingness to gamble. . .'

'At this moment you'd like to take a gamble and be transported into a world of sensual delight. But you're scared stiff, and I can't help but wonder why.'

WE HOPE you're enjoying our new addition to our Contemporary Romance series—stories which take a light-hearted look at the Zodiac and show that love can be written in the stars!

Every month you can get to know a different combination of star-crossed lovers, with one story that follows the fortunes of a hero or a heroine when they embark on the romance of a lifetime with somebody born under another sign of the Zodiac. This month features a sizzling love-affair between **SAGITTARIUS** and **GEMINI**.

To find out more fascinating facts about this month's featured star sign, turn to the back pages of this book. . .

ABOUT THIS MONTH'S AUTHOR

Lee Wilkinson is an Aries, born on April the tenth. She is typically over-emotional, feeling rather than thinking, with a love of life and movement. Untypically she is something of an introvert, who hates to wear bright colours. Theoretically she would be happy being a hermit, but she likes people as individuals and usually has a houseful. Her family, including the dog, are very important to her. Impatient and enthusiastic, she has a tendency to want to run the world, and frequently terrifies her loved ones by rushing in where angels fear to tread.

Recent titles by the same author:

MY ONLY LOVE

JOY BRINGER

BY

LEE WILKINSON

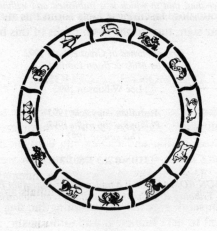

MILLS & BOON LIMITED
ETON HOUSE   18–24 PARADISE ROAD
RICHMOND   SURREY   TW9 1SR

All the characters in this book have no existence outside the imagination of the Author, and have no relation whatsoever to anyone bearing the same name or names. They are not even distantly inspired by any individual known or unknown to the Author, and all the incidents are pure invention.

All Rights Reserved. The text of this publication or any part thereof may not be reproduced or transmitted in any form or by any means, electronic or mechanical, including photocopying, recording, storage in an information retrieval system, or otherwise, without the written permission of the publisher.

This book is sold subject to the condition that it shall not, by way of trade or otherwise, be lent, resold, hired out or otherwise circulated without the prior consent of the publisher in any form of binding or cover other than that in which it is published and without a similar condition including this condition being imposed on the subsequent purchaser.

First published in Great Britain 1992 by Mills & Boon Limited

© Lee Wilkinson 1992

Australian copyright 1992 Philippine copyright 1992 This edition 1992

ISBN 0 263 77803 7

STARSIGN ROMANCES is a trademark of Harlequin Enterprises B.V., Fribourg Branch. Mills and Boon is an authorised user.

Set in 10 on 11 pt Linotron Times 01-9211-56684 Z

Typeset in Great Britain by Centracet, Cambridge Made and printed in Great Britain

CHAPTER ONE

THE small jet came in to land with a rush at Marco Polo Airport and, brakes squealing a protest, taxied clear of the runway.

With eager anticipation, though her clear golden-brown eyes held a hint of sadness, Luce Weston descended the steps.

She'd always wanted to travel—influenced by her Sagittarian star sign, Aunt Maureen claimed—but, owing to circumstances, this was the first real chance she'd had.

'Next year we'll take some time off and go to Italy together,' her mother had said. 'You'll absolutely adore Venice.'

But there had been no "next year" for Luce Weston senior.

Heat struck through the thin soles of her sandals as, joining the straggling file of other passengers, Luce made her way across the tarmac towards the rather unprepossessing terminal building.

Though late afternoon, it was like walking into a blast furnace and she was glad she'd twisted her dark, glossy hair into a knot on top of her head.

'It sure as hell is *hot*,' Dolly Cook remarked to Luce. 'I told Walt he'd never stand the heat, but he wouldn't listen.'

Middle-aged, plump and perspiring, the garrulous American couple who were "doing Europe" had been sitting next to Luce on the flight from London.

Appreciating their friendliness, she had smiled and listened to them talk practically non-stop throughout the entire journey.

5

6 JOY BRINGER

The few formalities over, she gathered up her luggage and made her way outside into the baking sun. A group of young men were gathered by the door. One wolf-whistled stridently, the rest looked her over in insolent silence.

According to her mother, Italian males were inveterate lookers. But, having been blessed with long, slender legs and what Paul described as a model-girl's figure, she was used to being stared at, so she walked past them with her normal slightly coltish grace, her composure intact.

There was no sign of any taxis, so Luce bought a book of tickets and boarded the already packed bus for the thirteen-kilometre drive to the city.

She was forced to stand at the back, squashed between a thin jeans-clad youth with bony shoulders and sharp elbows and a red-faced man with a paunch. Each time the driver braked or accelerated violently she was thrown off balance, barking her shins on various pieces of luggage.

The coastal strip was flat and uninteresting, the juddering vehicle hot and noisy, and she breathed a heartfelt sigh of relief when they reached the long bridge linking Venice with the mainland.

It was her first sight of the city, and it was magical. She drew in a deep breath as its domes and spires appeared, floating serene and enchanted, insubstantial as any mirage in the shimmering air.

None of these epithets fitted the Piazzale Roma, however. This was the terminus, no vehicles went beyond it, but were left either in huge public car parks or blocks of private garages. The large square was crowded, dusty and clamorous and full of diesel fumes and the smell of fried onions.

The bus ground to a halt alongside an open stall selling fruit and cold drinks and thin white slices of

JOY BRINGER

fresh coconut arranged in a fan shape beneath a sparkling jet of water.

Luce felt a wreck. Both stockings were laddered, her hair had started to come down, and her new floral suit, which had looked so smart in London, was sticking to her.

Brushing her wispy fringe away from her hot forehead, she settled the strap of her bag over her shoulder and, taking her case in one hand and her grip in the other, struggled off the bus.

When she had booked herself a room the clerk had suggested taking either a water-taxi or a *vaporetto* to the hotel.

Moving out of the path of the crowd, she put her luggage down on the uneven pavement and looked around.

Perhaps she *should* have let Signor Candiano arrange her accommodation and meet her. But his insistence that she leave everything to him had only served to strengthen her determination to be independent.

A determination born recently of Paul's excessive zeal to cosset and take care of her. . .

Her thoughts were interrupted by the sight of a man. He was standing aloof, black-haired, broad-shouldered and narrow-hipped, taller than the average Italian, an air of contained, but absolute authority setting him apart from the noisy, gesticulating mob.

Despite the casual modern clothes he wore, he looked as if he'd stepped from some early-Renaissance painting. His was a dark, autocratic face, with clear-cut features that held an austere masculine beauty.

He glanced in her direction and she was startled to see that his eyes, instead of being dark, were silvery pale and piercing.

She experienced a strong feeling of *déjà vu*, as if she'd seen him before, as if she *knew* him. But it wasn't so.

8   JOY BRINGER

For no reason at all, she shivered and dropped her gaze.

When, drawn by a magnetism she was unable to resist, she looked his way again, he was gone, the place where he'd been standing now occupied by a stout lady in an unbecoming striped sundress.

Luce felt an overwhelming sense of loss, and for a moment or two could only stand there, stunned by her extreme reaction to a total stranger.

Rousing herself, she glanced at the huge diamond solitaire on her left hand as if for reassurance, before picking up her luggage and heading for the steps which led down to the landing-stage and the *vaporetti*.

The Grand Canal was wider than she'd anticipated, teeming with water-buses and motorboats, barges and gondolas. Picturesque and colourful in pastel hues, it was lined on either side with baroque and rococo churches, pale marble *palazzos* and beautiful old buildings.

Luce stood by the rail, a cooling breeze fanning her cheeks and lifting her fringe and the loose tendrils of dark hair. Sun glinted off the water and the golden light was so pellucid, so dazzling, that she felt in her bag for her sunglasses.

Though almost as crowded as her previous transport, the water-bus was a great deal more pleasant. Her love of life and colour making all her perceptions jewel-bright, Luce thoroughly enjoyed her journey down Venice's main thoroughfare.

When they had passed under the Ponte di Rialto, with a disappointing view of the backs of its double row of shops, she checked the directions given to her by the hotel clerk, and, along with a jostling crowd of people, some tourists, some locals, disembarked at Sant'Angelo.

A glimpse of a tall black-haired man on the edge of the throng sent sudden excitement sky-rocketing. Dis-

JOY BRINGER

tracted, Luce stubbed her toe against a piece of raised planking and tripped. When she regained her balance and looked around he—if indeed it had been *he*—had vanished. She found herself struggling against a bitter, unreasonable disappointment.

Hotel Trevi was some five minutes' walk away in a quiet backwater. The main entrance was on a small, dusty square grandly named Campo San Pietro, while, at the rear, steps led down to a canal and a private landing-stage for the guests arriving by water-taxi.

At first glance the hotel closely resembled a deserted factory, with narrow, shuttered windows and peeling stucco. But, once through the heavy smoked-glass entrance doors, Luce found it was surprisingly luxurious, with cool marble floors and crystal chandeliers.

As she approached the reception desk she saw that the Cooks were already there, apparently having trouble understanding something the short balding clerk was trying to explain.

'Can I help?' she asked.

'I sure hope so.' Walt took out a large coloured handkerchief and mopped his damp brow. 'Danged if I can get the hang of what he's saying.'

Turning to the clerk, Luce said, '*Io parlo Italiano*.'

A look of gratitude spreading over his face, the man burst into a fresh flood of speech.

'There's a problem over a double booking,' she translated. 'You're being offered a different room, one without a private bath. But there is a bathroom right next door.'

The Cooks agreed to the change, and, having thanked Luce, Walt asked, 'How come you speak this foreign lingo so fluently?'

'My mother came from Italy,' she told him.

'Well, what do you know!' Dolly exclaimed. 'I'd never have guessed, you've such a creamy complexion and your eyes are quite light. . . but then, I expect your father's English?'

'Yes, he was. Though I take after my mother in looks. Mamma was born in Mestre, quite close to here. It's mainly the southern Italians who have dark eyes and olive skins.'

Luce's room, with a terrazzo floor and the minimum of modern furniture, was at the back, looking over the canal. Going to the open window, she pushed the grey slatted shutters wider and peered out.

Low evening sun slanted across the oily water, making it the colour of pea soup, and lit up the crumbling brickwork of the building opposite. It wasn't much of a view. But then, she hadn't come to Venice to sit in a hotel room.

She took fresh undies, a red cotton dress, and a pair of open-toed court shoes from her case, and went into the adjoining bathroom. As soon as she'd freshened up she would go out for a meal and see something of the city and the people who lived here.

With that thought came a vivid picture of a lean, arresting face, the light, brilliant eyes in striking contrast to the black hair and brows. A strong, dark, classical face, with a cleft chin and that peculiarly haunting quality she'd seen only in the paintings of old masters.

A face that was poignantly familiar, as if she'd always carried a picture of him in her heart. A face she longed to see again.

But of course he might not live here. He could be merely a visitor. Yet intuitively she felt convinced he wasn't. He *belonged* here, fitted so well with Venice's proud past. She could quite easily imagine him in a black cloak or a doge's zoia.

Unconsciously she sighed.

Then, feeling oddly guilty, as if just thinking about

JOY BRINGER

another man was betraying Paul, she pushed the romantic picture away.

Refreshed by a cool shower, her cloud of dark hair loose around her shoulders, she left the hotel and, following the signs, began to make her way through an absolute rabbit-warren of narrow streets towards Piazza San Marco.

Bordered on three sides by palatial arcades, and faced on the other by the Basilica of St Mark, the huge square seemed to be the hub of Venice.

Sunday evening being no exception, its open-air cafés were crowded. Music, talk and laughter swirled and eddied, while perfume, cigar smoke and the aroma of roasting coffee mingled with a warm salt breeze from the lagoon.

As Luce strolled past one of the restaurants a small table became free.

Having ordered a seafood salad, she sipped a glass of dry white wine and listened to the orchestra playing Neapolitan love-songs while the sun set and the lanterns came on, glowing a weird purple in the warm blue dusk.

All the time she watched the passing crowd, hoping to catch a glimpse of one certain face. A fascinating face with clearly drawn features that were indelibly printed on her memory.

Gradually, as she lingered over her coffee, the sky became an indigo canopy and a thick layer of cloud moved stealthily in from the Adriatic to obscure the moon and blot out the stars.

It was getting late when, prompted by the thought of having to start work next morning, she paid her bill and reluctantly set off back to the hotel.

As soon as she left the main tourist route it became quieter and darker. Very much darker.

At first she walked with confidence, reversing her

earlier directions, but after a while she began to get confused.

Where the narrow alleys crossed and re-crossed, street names were fastened to the walls at just above head-height, but without light she was unable to read them, and there wasn't a soul about to ask.

Reaching yet another intersection, she hesitated momentarily. But surely she turned right here into a small square?

Yes, through the gloom she could just make out the dried-up fountain in the middle of it, and, straight ahead, the huge studded doors of a church.

A couple of streets beyond that should be the canal that ran behind the hotel and, some hundred yards along the *fondamenta*, the bridge that led to Campo San Pietro.

After several minutes had passed without her finding a familiar landmark, Luce realised she must have gone wrong somewhere and tried to double back. Almost immediately she was forced to admit she was lost.

This area was an absolute maze of alleys, black and deserted. Not even a shuttered window was to be seen, just the barred doors and high, featureless walls of what she guessed were mainly warehouses.

She felt, and determinedly ignored, the first disturbing pricks of fear.

Hardly able to see a hand in front of her, but refusing to be daunted, Luce moved as fast as she dared down an alley-way little more than a metre wide. The air seemed dank and strangely chill, and her footsteps echoed eerily in the silence.

Sensing rather than seeing something lying in her path, she stopped abruptly. She had just identified the object as a large flat piece of cardboard when she realised that footsteps behind her had carried on. Stealthy footsteps, effectively masked by hers while she'd kept walking.

JOY BRINGER

As she listened the furtive sounds ceased. All she could hear was her own ragged breathing and the thud of her heart.

The fine hairs on the back of her neck rose. This was no ordinary passer-by, someone she could appeal to for help. Whoever was there was stalking her!

Blind panic sent her off at a stumbling run.

She'd gone only a short way when some sixth sense brought her to a halt in the nick of time. The alley ended abruptly in a couple of steps leading down to the sluggish black waters of a canal.

Her spine pressed against the rough bricks of one of the walls, she stared back the way she'd come. There wasn't a sound, yet she was convinced that close by in the darkness someone lay in wait.

Someone who knew she was trapped.

Despite the stifling fear, her brain was working furiously. She couldn't swim, so that left her with only two options: she could stay where she was and wait for whoever was lurking there to reach out of the darkness—but with her nature that was unthinkable—or she could run the gauntlet. He wouldn't be expecting that and, if he didn't hear her coming, the element of surprise might enable her to get past him.

Not giving her resolve time to weaken, she slipped off her shoes and hurtled up the alley as fast as she could go.

She was right at the end when, without warning, she ran full tilt into the arms of the waiting figure. Luce heard the man give a little grunt, while at the same instant the impact drove most of the breath from her body.

He was tall and sinewy, and his fingers gripped her arms with a steely strength. Sobbing for breath, she struck out at him, fighting desperately to free herself.

'It's all right.' He spoke crisply in cultured English.

14 JOY BRINGER

'There's no need to panic. *Hold still*. I'm not intending to do you any harm.'

As soon as she stopped struggling and stood motionless he let her go and bent to pick up the shoes she'd dropped.

'You'd better put these back on.'

When she straightened up he handed her her bag.

'Nor am I intending to rob you.'

But when, clutching the bag, she made an attempt to brush past him he blocked her way, adding coldly, 'It's not safe to be roaming around the back-streets on your own at this time of night. You could walk into a canal. Or worse. Surely you realise that?'

Luce tried to speak, but all that emerged was a strangled croak. Standing so close, she was aware of a faint scent of expensive aftershave, and his shirt had felt like silk.

Her common sense told her that this was no ruffian. Yet she wished fervently that she could see his face, *see* what kind of man he was.

His voice brusque rather than sympathetic, he observed, 'You're shaking like a leaf. It's no doubt the shock. Come along with me—you need a brandy.'

Oddly reassured by that very lack of sympathy, Luce followed him on legs that felt as if they hardly belonged to her. Almost at once she stumbled.

Taking her arm, he slowed his pace a little, but still he moved through the darkness with the absolute confidence of some night creature.

So quickly that she could scarcely credit it, they emerged into a well-lit square where several open-air cafés were still busy.

When the light from a lamp fell full on that dark, austere face she gasped, momentarily convinced that her brain was playing tricks.

He gave her a swift glance from those pale, brilliant eyes, but said nothing.

JOY BRINGER

Beneath the casual silk shirt his shoulders were even wider than she'd thought, and he was taller. But he was undoubtedly the man who had made such a powerful impact on her in the Piazzale Roma.

Despite the warmth of the night, Luce was still shivering. Steering her to the nearest free table, he disappeared inside the café, to return almost at once with two brandies.

Her hand shook as she lifted the glass to her lips, and, unused to spirits, she coughed as the fiery liquor burnt its way down her throat.

Having watched in silence while she drank most of it, he observed, 'Your colour's coming back now.'

His English was perfect, with no trace of an accent, so he was almost certainly a visiting businessman who knew the city well, rather than a Venetian, as she'd fondly imagined.

Frowning a little, he demanded, 'What were you doing, roaming around the back-streets in the dark?'

Finding her voice at last, and reacting to his disapproving tone, she retorted, 'What were you doing, following me?'

'Following you?' He raised a sardonic brow. 'What makes you think I was following you?'

'Weren't you?' she challenged.

'Do I look like a mugger or a potential rapist?' He let his amusement be apparent.

Feeling foolish now, she said, 'Well, I heard footsteps behind me and. . .'

'Jumped to the rather melodramatic conclusion that someone was following you?'

'But, after *I* stopped, *they* stopped.' She shuddered at the memory.

'In those narrow alley-ways sounds carry strangely and can be very misleading, especially at night.'

When, knowing she had a tendency to dramatise

things, she said nothing, he added, 'Tomorrow you'll be able to laugh about it.'

'I'm not sure my sense of humour's that good.'

'Well, if it's as good as your imagination. . . Tell me, if you're so nervous, why were you wandering about alone?'

'I'm not usually nervous, and I wasn't wandering about. I was trying to find the way back to my hotel, but I got hopelessly lost.'

'Not hopelessly, I assure you.' His tone was dry. Indicating one of the wider streets leading off the square, he added, 'A short walk down Calle Lunga brings you to the Grand Canal.'

After studying her for a moment in silence, he added, 'What possessed you to take off your shoes and come charging out of the alley like that?'

When, feeling even more foolish, she'd given her explanation Luce forced herself to look up at him.

Expecting to see only derision in those clear, light eyes, she was surprised to find they held a flicker of unwilling respect, even admiration, but all he said was, 'Would you like another brandy?'

She shook her head.

'A coffee perhaps?'

'I'd love a coffee.' Though the time she was spending with this man could hardly be described as comfortable, she didn't want it to end.

He signalled a waiter who was lounging in the doorway, and gave the order in Italian that sounded as fluent as his English, before continuing, 'So, what brings you to Venice?'

Tearing her gaze away from that clear-cut mouth with a bottom lip that made butterflies dance in her stomach, she asked hurriedly, 'Perhaps you've heard of Peter Sebastian?'

'Should I have?'

'He's an artist of exceptional talent, a painter as well

as a sculptor. I understand he's done quite a lot of his work in Venice.'

Getting no response, she went on a shade breathlessly, 'I've come here to do a *catalogue raisonné*, and help make the arrangements for mounting an exhibition of his sculpture.'

For a long time now Luce had been a great admirer of Peter Sebastian's work, and had been over the moon when she'd been approached and offered this wonderful opportunity.

'So you know the city fairly well?'

'No, I don't really know Venice at all.'

Those disturbing eyes on her face, he pressed, 'But you've been before, Miss. . .?'

'Weston. . .Luce Weston,' she supplied, adding, 'No, this is my first visit. My first time abroad, in fact.'

She could sense a sudden, incomprehensible anger in the man opposite that totally threw her. Stammering a little, she said the only thing she could think of. 'Y-you haven't told me your name.'

The anger, if that was what it had been, was swiftly masked. Urbanely he responded, 'Forgive me, I'm forgetting my manners. My name is. . .' the hesitation was almost imperceptible '. . .Michele Lorenzo.'

'Oh,' she said, 'I thought you were English.'

'No, I'm Italian.'

It was odd that he'd first spoken to her in English when he couldn't possibly have known. . .

She abandoned the half-formed thought as he went on, 'I was educated in England, and lived there for a number of years. But I'm Venetian by birth.' The last words, though spoken without undue emphasis, clearly showed his pride in his heritage.

With a rush of emotion she couldn't put a name to Luce realised that her first instinctive feeling about him had been absolutely right.

She swallowed. 'Then you live in Venice?'

18   JOY BRINGER

'My home is here. Though I have world-wide business interests which entail quite a lot of travelling.'

'Lucky you.'

He agreed, 'I think so. If I stay in the same place for too long I get stale.'

At that moment the coffee arrived, and as Luce opened a pack of sugar and stirred it in he remarked, 'I see you're engaged, Miss Weston.' His voice had an edge like a whetted knife.

She glanced at her left hand as if she'd forgotten the fact, and was instantly ashamed to find herself wishing she hadn't been wearing the showy diamond solitaire. 'Yes, I. . .'

'Does your fiancé also belong to the art world?'

'No, he's a civil engineer.'

Blond and beefy, built like a rugby forward, Paul had a very straightforward approach to life and a cheerful disregard, almost contempt, for anything remotely "artistic".

Since her mother's death he'd made himself practically indispensable. On an emotional and spiritual 'low', she had accepted, and been grateful for, his advice, his support, his protection.

Then he'd begun pressing her to marry him.

Luce had tried to tell him she wasn't sure enough of her feelings, but Paul was like a human bulldozer. Handsome, confident, knowing exactly what he wanted, and what she *ought* to want, it had been hard— no, virtually *impossible* in her depressed state—to hold out against him.

'What's your fiancé's name?' Michele Lorenzo's cold eyes pinned her.

'Paul Jenkins.'

'Have you been engaged for long?'

Luce felt a strong disinclination to talk about her engagement, and answered offhandedly, 'No, not very long.'

JOY BRINGER

A glance at her companion made her feel as if she'd been slapped. He was looking at her with an icy contempt.

Had she offended his sense of propriety by sounding dismissive, uncaring about her engagement?

'Have you ever been engaged before?' The bleakness of his gaze alarmed and unnerved her.

'Why. . .why do you ask?'

'Have you?'

'No. . .no, I haven't,' she lied, unable to confess her youthful folly to this grim-faced man.

There was a lengthening silence. He broke it to say abruptly, 'It's getting very late.' Then, with distant civility, 'Perhaps you'll allow me to see you safely to your hotel?'

'Thank you.'

They had just risen to their feet when a strident voice exclaimed, 'Well, will you look who's here. . .?'

Dolly Cook, her husband in tow, was descending on them. She beamed at Luce. 'I guess you've been seeing all the sights, same as we have? I just said to Walt, we ought to be getting a gon-doh-lar back.' Her glance lingered with open curiosity on the tall black-haired man by Luce's side.

Good manners demanding it, Luce made the formal introduction, adding perforce, 'Mr and Mrs Cook are staying in the same hotel.'

Suddenly appearing very Italian, Michele Lorenzo gave the American couple a polite little bow. '*Signore, signora.* . . I hope you'll find your visit to *Venezia* most enjoyable. *Buona notte.*'

To Luce he said, 'Since you've no further need of my services, Miss Weston, I'll bid you goodnight also,' and turned to go.

She wanted desperately to catch hold of his arm, to stop him walking out of her life. But convention prevented her. She stood staring after his lithe figure,

JOY BRINGER

gripped by the same sense of anguish and loss that she'd felt in the *Piazzale Roma*.

Not without some sensitivity, Dolly exclaimed, 'I sure hope we didn't break anything up?'

'Of course not.' To her credit, Luce's voice was steady. She even managed a smile.

Dolly sighed gustily. 'My, isn't he just *handsome*? Have you known him long?' Her round blue eyes gleamed with eager speculation.

Luce shook her head. 'We'd only just met. Stupidly I got lost trying to find my way back to the hotel and Signor Lorenzo came to my assistance.'

Anxious to change the subject, she added, 'If you were intending to get a gondola. . .?'

In the event they had to make do with a water-taxi. Feeling oddly bereft and desolate, besieged by Dolly's incessant chatter, Luce was pleased to get back to the hotel.

When she reached her room and bent to open the door the key stubbornly refused to turn. She was just wondering if she'd been given the wrong one when she realised that the door wasn't locked.

But surely she'd locked it? She recalled the grating noise the key had made.

Frowning a little, she let herself in and looked around. Everything was as she'd left it, her case untouched.

No, not untouched. Her nerves abruptly tightened and her heartbeat quickened. That striped blouse hadn't been lying on top.

A quick check showed that someone had undoubtedly searched through her belongings. Yet nothing appeared to be missing. The large oval locket that had been an eighteenth-birthday present from her aunt, a gold bracelet, a pair of drop earrings and—she breathed a sigh of relief—her mother's clip were still in the sandalwood box her parents had given her.

The curiously shaped clip was the most precious of the lot, and Luce's favourite. It was formed in a small oblong, one side rounded, the other almost straight.

An unusual and exquisite piece of work in gold and enamel, it depicted what was undoubtedly a white unicorn against a blue shield. What made it exceptional was that, in place of the single horn, a gold arrow pointed into the sky.

Surely any thief would have taken that?

Then who had gone through her things?

There were fresh towels in the bathroom, so the likeliest explanation was a nosy chambermaid.

Somewhat reassured, Luce cleaned her teeth and climbed into bed.

Slipping off her ring, she put it on the bedside cabinet with an inward sigh. After managing to hold out for several months against Paul's pressurising, she had agreed to the engagement only a few days before this trip.

It was the fact that she would be away for six weeks or more that had brought things to a head. He'd been unhappy at her leaving without some commitment, anxious that she should have the "protection" of his ring on her finger.

But perhaps she should have paid more heed to her Aunt Maureen. . .

Maureen Weston was an intelligent, forthright woman. Since her brother's death two years before she'd worked with her sister-in-law and niece in Ventura, their London art gallery. Then, nine months ago, when Luce Weston senior had been killed in a motorway pile-up, she had, at her niece's request, taken over the running of the gallery.

Still a beautiful woman at turned fifty, Maureen was a spinster from choice, and had strong views on the subject of relationships.

JOY BRINGER

'Paul's not the right one for you, any more than Dave was. . .' she'd said bluntly.

Dave had been Luce's first serious boyfriend. At eighteen, in love with love, she'd accepted his ring and walked on air until common sense had brought her down to earth and made her realise that marriage to him would be a total disaster.

'. . .you've only got to look at his star sign.'

'Rubbish!' Luce had exclaimed. 'I might read my horoscope in the daily paper, but I've no intention of letting astrology rule my life.'

Maureen had given her an exasperated look. 'I'm not suggesting you should. But it can help us to understand ourselves, and give a useful insight into other people.

'You're impulsive, creative, a joyous, intuitive type of Sagittarian. Paul's a down-to-earth Taurean, a marvellous man for the right woman. But he won't understand your love of colour and excitement, your need to dream, and he'll stifle you with his possessiveness. . . Besides, you don't love him.'

'I'm very fond of him.'

'You may be *fond* of him, but that's not enough. You ought to find someone on the same wavelength, who knows your mind, your love of freedom, who thinks of you the same instant you think of him. Someone who is so much a *part* of you that if you were separated you'd no longer feel whole.'

Luce moved restlessly and thumped her pillow, her doubts and uncertainties back in full force; and all because she'd met a man who had captured her interest and set her imagination winging.

A man who was in all probability married and with a family. Italians, so her mother had said, tended to settle young. Michele Lorenzo must be at least thirty-two or -three, so it was unlikely that he was still single. . .

And what possible difference could it have made if they were both free? Though he'd scarcely taken his eyes off her, it was obvious that she hadn't made a very favourable impression on him.

In any case, he hadn't asked where she was staying, and she had no idea where he lived. Admittedly, Venice wasn't a very big place, but the odds on their meeting again by chance were minimal.

Yet she knew for certain that if she never saw him again she would never forget him. His physical impact had been so strong.

But it was more than just a physical thing. Much more. It was as though her soul had looked beyond the flesh and instantly recognised its counterpart.

Sentimental claptrap, Luce scolded herself. But, more shaken than she cared to admit, it was a long time before she slept.

CHAPTER TWO

IN THE middle of the night that warning sense which safeguarded sleepers sounded an alarm, scattering Luce's dreams. She wakened as though from some disaster, bewildered, more than a little frightened.

Lying quite still, trying to recall whether, with her mind so busy, she'd remembered to lock the door, she listened. Yes, there it was again, a stealthy sound, quite close at hand.

Sitting up abruptly, she demanded, 'Who's there?'

She sensed rather than saw a movement. Heart racing, she felt for the dangling cord and flooded the room with light just as the door closed quietly.

Jumping out of bed, she peered into the dimly lit corridor. It was silent and deserted.

Paul's ring was on the bedside cabinet, where she'd placed it, and her handbag. . . Her handbag was lying open.

Had she left it open? She didn't think so, but she wasn't absolutely sure.

Snatching it up, Luce checked the contents. Her purse, containing a few thousand lire, was still there; so were her traveller's cheques and credit cards.

Nothing at all had been taken.

Had she been dreaming or, only half awake, imagined the intruder? Yet again she couldn't be certain.

Having locked the door, she climbed back into bed and, turning off the light, willed herself to relax. But it was quite a while before her heartbeat returned to normal and she began to feel calm again.

As soon as she closed her eyes a dark, austerely handsome face filled her mind, crowding out the last of

24

JOY BRINGER   25

her lingering fright, and when she eventually managed
to get back to sleep it was to dream of Michele Lorenzo
once more.

Luce became aware of sunlight lying like a warm
caress across her closed lids, and opened her eyes to
find the shutters throwing tiger stripes of light and
shade across the bed.

She awakened with a feeling of anticipation, of
urgency almost. A feeling of things to be done,
decisions to be made.

But while she had slept one decision had already
been made: she couldn't marry Paul. All her previous
doubts as to whether they were right for each other,
whether she cared for him enough, had been answered
by her reaction to Michele Lorenzo. If a stranger could
have such an effect on her she should never have agreed
to wear Paul's ring.

Now that she knew for certain that she couldn't
marry him, her first impulse was to call him up and tell
him so. It wasn't fair to leave him in a fool's paradise,
and for her own peace of mind she wanted to have
everything settled.

She had sat up and stretched out a hand to lift the
receiver when she paused. Honest, impatient with any
kind of pretence, it went against the grain to dissemble,
but she couldn't end their brief engagement with a
phone call. She must wait and see Paul, talk to him face
to face.

But before she could do that, she thought, jumping
out of bed and heading for the bathroom, she had a job
to tackle. A job she was looking forward to
enormously.

Signor Candiano's letter had come out of the blue.
Written in careful English, it had told her little except
that her name had been suggested to him by a Kevin
Roberts, who had tutored briefly at her old art school,
and knew their London gallery.

Hardly daring to believe her good fortune, Luce had heaped blessings on the man she scarcely remembered, and jumped at the chance.

Some twenty minutes later, cool and attractive in a tangerine and white suit, dark, gleaming hair coiled neatly on top of her head, she went down to the desk. There she asked to have Paul's ring put in the hotel's safe and, that done, walked away with a sense of relief.

The breakfast-room was half empty as yet, pleasant and airy with green plants and whirring fans. Sitting by a potted palm that looked like a fugitive from the desert, she ate flaky rolls spread with black cherry jam, and drank two cups of coffee before setting forth.

Outside the light was dazzling, the sky as blue as lapis lazuli. Though it was barely nine o'clock, sun blazed down, and already the huge slabs of stone paving the *campo* threw back an oven heat. As yet, very few people were about, the majority of holiday-makers still at breakfast.

Following the directions she'd been sent, Luce reached Calle Nerone in about fifteen minutes. With an air of picturesque decay, the street, little more than an alley, lay dusty and deserted, well away from the tourist area.

Her goal proved to be a tall, thin building, leaning like an amiable drunk, supported by its neighbours. The old wooden door, leading to a bare lobby, was standing wide.

Fascinated to find that the floor, ceiling, and walls all sloped at crazy angles, Luce climbed the rickety stairs to Signor Candiano's office.

The agent came forward to meet her, a short, plump man, nattily dressed, with thinning hair and a black moustache. Though he greeted her in good English, he looked curiously ill at ease, his brown eyes repeatedly sliding away from hers.

After enquiring about her journey and whether the

JOY BRINGER

hotel was comfortable, he said abruptly, 'I have another appointment shortly, so it might be best to take you straight over to the *palazzo*, where you will be working.'

Having expected a leisurely discussion, Luce was surprised by the brevity of this first meeting. It was almost as if the agent couldn't get rid of her fast enough. But, turning obediently, she led the way down the stairs and out into the bright heat of the day.

A narrow *rio* ran past the bottom of Calle Nerone, and waiting by some steps was a small boat. Having helped her in, Signor Candiano turned the key and the engine spluttered into life.

As, apparently disregarding the speed limit, they sped through a network of small canals lined on either side by the backs of tall buildings Luce enquired, 'The *palazzo* you mentioned. . .what is it called?'

The man at the wheel appeared not to have heard. A moment or so later, with evident relief, he said, 'Here we are.'

To their left, set into a wall made from massive blocks of stone and lapped by greeny-blue water, were the huge wooden doors of a boat-house. They were closed, but just beyond them he cut the engine and drew up to a short flight of steps with a small studded door at the top.

It wasn't at all what Luce had expected, and, seeing her puzzled frown, he said hastily, apologetically, 'I hope you do not mind using the rear entrance, but I needed to go this way to get to my next appointment.'

'No, of course I don't mind,' she assured him, adding, 'Where exactly are we?'

Making no reply, the agent tied up to an iron ring let into the stone. Surprisingly light and nimble, he jumped out and extended a hand to help her from the rocking boat.

To the right of the door dangled a piece of chain. He

28 JOY BRINGER

jerked it a couple of times, and somewhere inside the cavernous depths a bell jangled loudly.

Luce was about to ask a second time where they were when the door was opened by a plump, middle-aged woman wearing a neat black dress.

'This is Miss Weston,' Signor Candiano announced. Then to Luce, 'Rosa—the housekeeper—will take care of you.'

Without further ado he hurried back down the steps.

Luce heard the engine start and the boat roar away as she obeyed Rosa's respectful injunction to, 'Please come this way.'

It was dim and pleasantly cool inside the *palazzo* as the housekeeper led the way along a bare passage, past what seemed to be mainly old kitchens and store-rooms, and up a flight of stone steps. At the top an arched door opened into a grand marble hall with an elegant horseshoe staircase.

As, heels clicking on the polished slabs, Luce followed the black-clad figure through the shuttered gloom she remarked, 'I haven't discovered what the *palazzo* is called, or who owns it. Perhaps you can tell me?'

Receiving no answer, and wondering if the woman had understood, she was about to repeat the question in Italian when Rosa opened one of several handsomely carved doors and ushered her into a large sitting-room.

In welcome contrast to the dimness and the heavy, ornate splendour that had gone before, the white ceiling and walls were unadorned and light poured in through several long windows.

It was a most attractive room, she thought, liking the simplicity of its amber-coloured carpet and comfortable modern furniture.

'. . .be with you shortly.'

Luce caught only the tail-end of Rosa's murmur as the housekeeper slipped out, closing the door quietly behind her.

JOY BRINGER

Wonderful! she thought. Not only was she still ignorant of which *palazzo* she was in, or where it was, but she also didn't even know the name of the person she was waiting for.

Walking over to the nearest window, she peered out and found herself looking across what was unmistakably the Grand Canal. Well, there was the answer to one question at least.

The others followed close on the heels of the first.

'Good morning, Miss Weston.'

She turned to find that a tall black-haired man, slimly built except for wide shoulders, had entered silently and was standing watching her. He was wearing a grey business suit, an immaculate white shirt and a red and grey striped silk tie.

Shocked into immobility, her heart racing with suffocating speed, she gaped at him stupidly as he added, 'Welcome to the Ca' del Leone.'

It was a moment or two before she was able to control the wild surge of emotion and say with commendable aplomb, 'Good morning, Signor Lorenzo. I didn't expect to meet you here.'

'So I gather.' His expression was sardonic.

Ruffled by it, her gladness was overlaid with vexation and she said crisply, 'You, on the other hand, *did* expect to meet me?'

'That's right.'

'May I ask why you didn't say anything when I explained what I was doing in Venice?'

He looked infuriatingly cool, unmoved by her imperfectly concealed annoyance, as he answered, 'I preferred our second meeting to be a surprise.'

Despite her love of the dramatic, Luce had never been over-keen on surprises. Often they turned out to be more like shocks, and she disliked the tension, the agitation, the feeling of disruption that frequently accompanied them.

30   JOY BRINGER

Repressively she said, 'Even as a child, I hated my jack-in-the-box.'

'Whereas I adored mine.' As if he was relishing the fact that she was disconcerted, his eyes held a glint of malicious satisfaction.

'Why did you want me to be at a disadvantage?' she demanded.

'Perhaps I just like having the advantage,' he returned silkily.

Clearly she was dealing with a master strategist. While she, as yet, didn't even know what kind of game they were playing, let alone the rules.

He was studying her, taking in the dark, silky fringe brushed to one side, the golden eyes, long and tilted upwards a little at the outer corners, the straight nose, the generous mouth with its full bottom lip, and the firm, if not to say stubborn, chin.

As she moved, restless beneath his scrutiny, with a mocking gesture he indicated one of the armchairs drawn up to the flower-filled fireplace. 'Won't you sit down?'

Her knees distinctly weak, she was glad to. As she sank back against the cushions a sleek black cat appeared from nowhere and began to wind itself around her ankles. 'Well, hello.' She stroked behind a velvet ear; the response was a loud purring.

There was a quick padding sound and a second cat jumped into her lap. Startled, she laughed. They were identical. Both jet black, both with bright green eyes.

'Castor and Pollux,' he told her, 'Cas and Poll for short. Do you like cats?'

'I like all animals. *Are* they twins?'

'Yes, I believe so. But far from heavenly. They have been known to bite and scratch on occasion. . . Come on, you two.' Opening a door to the left of the fireplace, he shooed the pair into the adjoining room.

Then, a lean index finger hovering over a bell-push,

JOY BRINGER 31

he asked, 'Would you like coffee, or lemon tea perhaps?'

She was dying for a coffee but some streak of perversity made her answer briskly, 'Neither, thank you. What I would like is to know something about the job I came here to do. Signor Candiano told me scarcely anything.'

'He was acting on my instructions,' her companion explained calmly.

Determined not to play into his hands, Luce bit back the curious questions, and simply waited.

He smiled, apparently entertained by her reluctance to be manipulated, and, taking a seat opposite, said, 'I, however, will tell you everything you need to know.'

It was the first time she'd seen him smile and, though it obviously wasn't *intended* to charm, it took her breath away and made her pulses quicken.

Silently instructing her mind to keep her physical reactions in check, she murmured, 'How very kind of you, Signor Lorenzo.'

Ignoring the sarcasm beneath the sugar coating, he went on smoothly, 'As we'll be working together, I hope you'll call me Michele.'

Ignoring the way her heart leapt and tumbled like a circus clown at the thought of working with him, *being* with him, she inclined her head. 'Very well.' Then, refusing to reciprocate, she sat with her hands clasped together lightly in her lap, trying to look at ease.

A slight lift of one winged brow the only sign that he was amused by her deliberate omission, he went on, 'Well, then, Luce—I may call you Luce?—what would you like to know?'

Trying not to reveal how very *aware* of him she was, she asked with a fair degree of composure, '*How* will we be working together?'

Again that malicious gleam. 'Amicably, I trust.'

Already she doubted it.

32 JOY BRINGER

'Perhaps if you tell me just where you stand?' she suggested shortly. 'I was under the impression that Signor Candiano was Peter Sebastian's agent, but possibly I'm mistaken and *you* are?'

'No.' His pale, brilliant eyes on her face, as if he was expecting some reaction, he said deliberately, 'I own Ca' del Leone.' Getting no response apart from polite interest, he pounced. 'Were you surprised to find yourself here again?'

Baffled, she frowned. 'As this is the first time I've been to Ca' del Leone, the answer must be no.'

'So you've never visited the *palazzo* before?' His question was sharp and cynical.

'As I told you last night, this is the only time I've ever been to Venice.'

He gave her a hard, penetrating look, a look that held a charge.

Puzzled and defensive, she wondered what he was accusing her of. Did he think she was lying for some reason? Refusing to make any further protestations, she set her lips and remained silent.

He was not only the most charismatic man she'd ever met, but also the most complex, aggravating, unaccountable, and arrogant. A difficult, not to say impossible, combination.

Could he be a Leo? His *palazzo* was called House of the Lion. . . Luce gave herself a mental shake. She was starting to pay an inordinate amount of attention to the star signs.

'You're not wearing your engagement-ring.'

Startled by his sudden, critical observation, she made a small gesture of dismissal. 'No. Does it matter?'

He stood up and towered over her, his silvery eyes blazing. 'It might to your fiancé. *Why* aren't you wearing it?'

She could have suggested that it was none of his business, or have made an excuse that she'd forgotten

JOY BRINGER

to put it on, but, wits scattered, with her usual honesty she blurted out the exact truth. 'I've decided that the engagement was a mistake.' It sounded bald and uncompromising.

His lips twisted. 'But you'll keep the ring?'

Her voice quivering with indignation, she answered, 'Of course I won't keep Paul's ring. As soon as I get home I shall give it him back.'

'Really?' As she stiffened at the implied doubt Michele rasped, 'I must congratulate you.'

'On what?' Her tone was distinctly frosty.

'On both your speed and skill.'

'I'm afraid I don't understand. . .'

'I presumed that you had another candidate—or should I say *victim*?—lined up.'

Taken aback by this vitriolic attack, Luce decided she'd had enough. A flush of anger on her high cheekbones, her honey-coloured eyes flashing, she jumped up. 'Signor Lorenzo, I consider your remarks not only uncalled for, but also extremely offensive. I've come here to do a job I very much want to do, but I refuse to stay and. . .'

At that moment the door to the next room, which had been left a little ajar, opened and a slim, petite woman came in, elegantly dressed in a blue crêpe de Chine suit that echoed the colour of her eyes. She was well into her thirties, nowhere near as young as the carefully styled fall of blonde hair suggested.

Her long nails were pearly pink, beautifully manicured, and Luce noticed she wore several rings, one of which looked like a wedding band.

In an accent that was unmistakably American she observed pleasantly, 'You must be Miss Weston. . . I'm Didi Lombard.'

Tiny and doll-like, she made Luce, who was five feet seven in flat sandals, feel like a giantess.

As the two women shook hands Didi added, 'I heard voices and thought I'd pop in to say hello.'

To Michele, who had risen to his feet, his dark face wiped clear of all expression, she said in rapid Italian, 'Do you think it's wise to antagonise our young friend? If she decides to go straight home all this will have been for nothing.'

There was a brief pause while the three stood like players who had forgotten their lines, then, turning to Luce, Michele said stiffly, 'I must ask you to forgive my unruly tongue and sense of humour.'

She was unable to believe that his tongue was unruly or that he'd meant his earlier remarks to be at all humorous.

With a formal little bow he added, 'Please accept my apologies.'

When she hesitated, hardly knowing what to say, he tipped the scales by proposing briskly, 'Perhaps we should get down to business. Would you care to see the items to be put on display?'

Their eyes met and, standing so close, she saw that his weren't grey, as she'd thought, but a clear silvery green, translucent as water. Eyes her soul could drown in.

Tearing her gaze away, she slid the strap of her bag over her shoulder and said in a tone she hoped was controlled and businesslike, 'Very well.'

Michele glanced at the blonde woman. 'Are you joining us, Didi?'

She wrinkled her dainty nose. 'No, thanks.' Smiling at Luce, she added, 'I run a gallery in New York, but at the moment I'm taking a holiday from the art world. See you later, Miss Weston.'

Putting a hand on Michele's sleeve with casual possessiveness, she spoke to him once again in Italian. 'I'm sure you'd get on better by being nice to the girl. You're a very attractive man and she's quite obviously

JOY BRINGER

smitten.' Her tone teasing, she added, 'If you went about it the right way I'm positive you could have her eating out of your hand in no time at all. *Caio, caro.*'

Obviously smitten, indeed! Resisting the urge to rout the pair of them by denying in Italian as fluent as theirs that she was any such thing, Luce kept her face impassive until the other woman had disappeared the way she'd come.

It would be less embarrassing if, without apparently knowing what had been said, she made it abundantly clear that Didi Lombard had been totally wrong, she *wasn't* smitten, and as for eating out of his hand. . .!

Michele moved to open the outer door, and asked levelly, 'Shall we go?'

As, her spine ramrod-straight, Luce accompanied him from the lived-in part of the *palazzo*, past grand salons and vaulted galleries, down to the basement regions thoughts wheeled and settled in her mind like swallows on a telegraph wire.

What made him think she'd visited the *palazzo* before? And why had he been so angry and contemptuous, so scathing about her broken engagement? Could he be a misogynist? If he was, how did the fair Didi fit into the picture? But, most puzzling of all, why was the American so anxious that he should be nice to her. . .?

'Here we are.'

Her thoughts taking flight, Luce found they had stopped halfway down a bare stone corridor.

Removing a key from his pocket, Michele unlocked a heavy wooden door with an eye-level grille, and, having switched on the light, unshered her inside.

It was a long windowless studio with neon strip-lighting set into the ceiling. There were several work-benches holding tools and various pieces of covered work, while shelving, tall cupboards and a low, flat sink took up the rest of the wall space.

36 JOY BRINGER

The furniture was meagre, consisting of a large deal desk, a single chair and a couple of tall stools. A door at the far end was a little ajar, showing that it led to a white-tiled wash-room.

When she'd had a moment or two to look around Michele said, 'Those are the items for exhibition.'

The deep shelves were packed with finished pieces of sculpture in a variety of different media—wood, stone, clay and metal—which bore the unmistakable stamp of Peter Sebastian's work.

Forgetting her earlier indignation, excitement bringing a sparkle to her golden eyes, Luce hurried over to look at them more closely.

They ranged from a tiny mouse, with lifelike whiskers and a twitchy nose, to a metre-high Pied Piper, whose grin was so wickedly triumphant that she almost expected to see the children of Hamlin following behind.

Then all at once Luce caught her breath. On the next shelf were twelve pieces of matching sculpture, each about twenty centimetres high. Though they weren't always the conventional portrayals, she had no difficulty in recognising that they represented the signs of the zodiac.

They were the most beautiful, sensuous things she'd ever seen, each one a perfect, magical work of art, displaying humour and pathos and poetry.

As befitted an earth sign, Taurus was made of clay, a sturdy little bull comically smelling a floret of clover.

The air sign, Gemini, was depicted by twin cats, ethereal in clear bluish glass, yet with an extra dimension because they were so clearly *communicating* with each other.

For a moment Luce had difficulty identifying Sagittarius; then she saw it was symbolised by its ruling planet, Jupiter, and was portrayed as the Bringer of Joy. Done in fiery bronze, it was a laughing child-woman, head thrown back, arms joyously outstretched. It *radiated* happiness.

Pisces, on the other hand, had an almost mystical quality. Caught in a green translucent wave were two tiny sea-horses facing in opposite directions, one frolicking, the other melancholy. It movingly captured the feeling of dual personality, of moods and emotional depths.

Turning a glowing face to her companion, Luce exclaimed, 'Aren't they *wonderful*?'

He gave a slight shrug. 'Some are better than others.'

'Does Peter Sebastian actually work here?'

'When he's in Venice.'

'Then you know him well?'

'Very well.'

'I've often wondered what he was like,' Luce admitted a shade wistfully. 'There's so little known about him. I was told he refuses point-blank to be photographed or give interviews.'

'He prefers his private life to remain private.'

There was a snap in the answer which made Luce say hurriedly, 'I don't blame him for that. But I believe until now he's never even agreed to hold a full-scale exhibition of his work?'

'Perhaps he's never felt the need.'

Michele was answering with a brevity that made it abundantly clear that he was disinclined to talk about the sculptor. But there was one more thing that Luce wanted to ask.

'I understand he's in the States at the moment. Do you think there's any chance of him coming back for the opening of——?'

A knock at the door interrupted her.

Michele went to answer, and Luce heard the murmur of voices before he turned to her and said, 'I'm afraid I must leave you. I'm wanted on the phone, and then I have a long-standing business lunch and a couple of other appointments.

'You'll find everything you need in either the desk or the cupboards.' Those light eyes rested on her as if he was making a mental sketch of her face; then he glanced at the slim gold watch on his wrist. 'It's almost twelve-thirty now. I'll have some sandwiches sent along.'

She was about to ask if he'd be back before she left for the night, when the door closed behind him.

Michele Lorenzo was without doubt the strangest, most complex man she'd ever met. She couldn't begin to understand him. He disconcerted her, baffled and enraged her, sparked off her fighting spirit.

But, despite everything, the strong physical attraction, the sense of *recognition*, the feeling of finding her soul's counterpart were all still there, powerful as ever. Perhaps she *was* smitten.

Well, if that was so she would need to work even harder to appear indifferent. She wouldn't humiliate herself by seeming to be drawn to a man who had appeared to dislike and distrust her on sight.

No, it was *more* than that.

Though he'd scarcely taken his eyes off her, and in a strange sort of way appeared to be fascinated by her, she sensed it was the kind of reluctant fascination one might feel for an intriguing, but poisonous snake.

There you go again, she scolded herself, over-dramatising things.

Still, it was true in the main, so for the few weeks she was to be in Venice she would take the greatest care to have as little to do with him as possible. That decided to her satisfaction, Luce felt more settled.

The minute she'd finished the ham sandwiches and coffee Rosa brought she began to examine and list the various pieces of sculpture, her thoughts still busy.

It would be wonderful if Peter Sebastian *did* come to Venice for the opening of his exhibition, though it had been suggested by the Press that he had an American fiancée, and might be staying permanently in the States. If he did it would be Europe's loss. His work was masterly.

Soon she was completely absorbed, and when she finally straightened and looked at her watch she was staggered to find it was getting on for six o'clock.

Not bad for the first day, she thought with a sense of satisfaction as she washed her hands and tucked in a few strands of escaping hair.

Having switched off the light, she locked the door and took the key with her. There wasn't a soul in sight nor a sound to be heard. The whole place seemed as empty and deserted as the Beast's magic castle, though she was certainly no Beauty, Luce thought ruefully.

Remembering the way Michele had brought her, she retraced her steps, not without a certain unease, a prickly feeling of discomfort, as though she was being watched by unseen eyes.

When she reached the wide passage that led to his apartment she hesitated. Apart from the finer details of the carving, which she hadn't stopped to note, all the doors looked alike. But surely it was the second on the right?

If no one was there she would just leave the key where he'd be sure to find it, and go. It would be a relief not to have to see him again tonight, Luce assured herself, ignoring an inner voice that jeered, Who are you trying to kid?

She tapped, and walked in to find not the sitting-room she'd expected, but a light, modern office.

Michele was sitting behind a leather-topped desk. He looked up from the papers he'd been working on and said blandly, 'Ah, Luce. . . I was about to come down and see where you'd got to.'

Silently she held out the key.

40   JOY BRINGER

'Thank you.' He accepted it. 'How is the work lining up?'

With an odd feeling that he was asking because it was expected of him rather than out of genuine interest, she replied somewhat stiltedly, 'Once I've a clear picture of the items to be displayed, and which room they're to go in, I can begin the first rough draft for the catalogue.'

'Very professional,' he congratulated her with a slightly crooked smile.

Before she could find a rejoinder to what, despite the smile, she felt sure was a snide remark he went on, 'If you're ready to leave now I'll take you back to your hotel.' As he spoke he rose to his feet.

He had changed out of his business suit, and now looked relaxed and elegant in casual off-white trousers and an olive-green shirt, open at the neck, showing a strong, tanned throat.

'Thank you, but that's quite unnecessary,' she assured him coolly. 'I can easily find my own way.'

He gave her a mocking glance from beneath long black lashes. 'As you did last night?'

'It was dark then.' Immediately she was annoyed with herself for sounding defensive.

'If you don't know Venice well it's quite possible to get lost even in broad daylight, and, as you don't speak Italian. . .' Perhaps something in her face alerted him because he stopped, then queried slowly, thoughtfully, 'Or *do* you?'

CHAPTER THREE

MICHELE'S silvery-green eyes seemed to look straight into her brain, and for what seemed minutes, but could only have been split-seconds, Luce stood paralysed, before shaking her head.

'Then I insist.'

He came round the desk and before she could form any further protest had taken charge. His hand firmly cupping her bare elbow, he escorted her through the door and along the passage.

When, pulses racing in a most disturbing manner, she tried to withdraw her arm his grip tightened, and he slanted her a glance from beneath long thick lashes that held a distinct challenge.

Luce debated stopping and having a showdown but, chickening out, she told herself it hardly seemed worth the hassle. Though she would take jolly good care not to let it happen again.

They crossed the marble hall to the main entrance with its massive metal-studded doors which, she judged, must have weighed tons. Michele turned a huge knob and, rather to her surprise, the left hand door swung open easily.

She blinked as they emerged into blinding brightness and searing heat, and paused to fumble for her sunglasses before they descended the broad flight of steps that led down to the canal.

To the right a small, bobbing motor-boat was moored to a black post. Having steadied it with his foot, Michele helped her in, stepped down lightly beside her, and brought the engine to life.

His wrists were muscular, she noted, and the tanned

41

42 JOY BRINGER

hands, with their neatly trimmed nails, strong and well shaped. Long-fingered, sensitive hands that held a seductive promise. . .

Averting her eyes, and mentally swatting the butter-flies her own erotic thoughts had set fluttering, Luce gazed around with interest while Michele named some of the more important buildings lining the canal's banks.

'This is Ca' del Serpente,' he told her as they drew level with a sinister-looking *palazzo*.

She could see where it got its name. Above an enormous door was coiled an immense stone serpent, evil head raised menacingly, ready to strike.

The *palazzo's* marble walls were made blotched and hideous by some obscene, scaly growth, and its steps were covered in green and black slime. The whole place had a hopeless air of neglect, a dead, decaying look.

It put Luce in mind of a corrupt and rotting corpse. She shivered.

Michele glanced at her.

'A pricking in my thumbs,' she said.

He nodded, so mentally close, so *aware* of what she was thinking and feeling, without being in the least sympathetic. 'With your imagination, it would get you that way. But when you see the inside. . .'

Ignoring his dig, she decided that if the inside was anything like the outside she could bear to wait. Forever.

As if she'd spoken the words aloud, he informed her, 'It's being renovated. The Save Venice trust are work-ing on it at the moment. In a matter of weeks, when it's opened to the public, it will look entirely different.'

'Will it *feel* any different?'

He grinned, deriding her patent lack of enthusiasm, and said ruthlessly, 'You'll have to brave it sooner or later.'

'Is a visit compulsory?'

JOY BRINGER

'If you want to carry on with your job.'

Light dawned. Faintly she said, 'The exhibition's being staged *there*? I thought. . .'

'I'm afraid I don't relish the idea of the general public tramping through my home.'

She flushed. 'No, stupid of me.'

'These old *palazzos* are often used as museums and exhibition centres. Some are even being turned into hotels.'

'You don't mind?'

He gave an expressive shrug. 'They're far too precious to our heritage for us to allow them to simply moulder away. . . The problem is, there's never enough money available.'

'I understand Peter Sebastian gives the trust a great deal of financial help,' Luce remarked.

'He can afford it,' Michele stated flatly.

Once again she got the distinct impression that he didn't want to talk about the sculptor.

She changed the subject. 'You remarked earlier that we would be working together, but you didn't specify *how*.'

He raised a dark brow.

'All you said was *amicably*,' she reminded him, her tone tart.

'And that doesn't appeal to you?' When she stayed silent he suggested, 'What about *closely*?'

Flustered, she looked away, but not before she'd caught the devilish gleam in his eyes.

Damn him! she thought crossly. How could she let herself be drawn to such an impossible man? But perhaps the question should be, how could she *stop* herself?

A little further on Michele turned into a side-canal, where it was shady and appreciably cooler. Wrought-iron balconies jutted out over the water, and high above their heads lines of washing were strung, hanging motionless in the hot, still air.

After passing beneath several narrow bridges, some wooden, some stone, under which Michele had to bend his head, they stopped at the intersection of two canals. Luce was about to ask why, when she noticed a set of traffic-lights.

As soon as the lights were in their favour they turned left, and after a short distance he cut the engine and they drew into a wooden landing-stage.

It took her a moment or two to realise they were at the hotel.

When he'd moored the boat and helped her out Michele followed her through the rear lobby and into the foyer. 'I'll wait for you here,' he remarked coolly.

'Wait for me?'

'While you shower and change before I take you out for a meal.'

She stiffened. 'There's really no need.'

'I agree there's no *need*, but I thought you might prefer to.'

She held on grimly to her temper. 'I mean, there's no need for you to take me out for a meal.'

His green eyes mocking, he asked, 'Isn't there?'

'If you're so concerned about me getting lost I can always eat in the hotel.'

Shaking his head, he said, 'It would be a shame to do that.' Then, with a smile that set all the butterflies off again, 'It's my intention to take you to where the food is really good, and also show you something of the city by night.'

His voice had been soft, his manner bland, but beneath the velvet veneer of politeness lay the cold steel of determination.

'That's very kind of you,' she capitulated, realising that any further argument would not only be useless, but also silly.

JOY BRINGER 45

As she made her way up to her room Luce wondered about him and his motives. Why was he insisting on escorting her? Had he decided to take Didi Lombard's advice? And if he *had*, what did he hope to gain by having her "eating out of his hand"?

She was in the shower when another, even more perplexing question suddenly popped into her mind. He hadn't asked where she was staying and she hadn't told him, so how had he known which hotel to bring her to?

Having deliberately taken her time, Luce descended the stairs some half an hour later, looking flower-fresh, her wispy fringe brushed to one side, her hair curling loosely on to her shoulders.

Pride had decreed she should put on her best white silky dress and—though her clear skin and dark brows and lashes needed little help from cosmetics—make-up with care.

Despite the lecture she'd been reading herself, excitement had put colour in her cheeks and made her clear golden-brown eyes sparkle.

As she reached the bottom step a slight fair-haired man, head down and hurrying, almost cannoned into her. She recoiled, and he caught her upper arms, steadying her.

'Sorry, and all that,' he said in English. 'I really ought to be more careful.' He looked and sounded genuinely apologetic.

He was about her own age, she guessed, nice-looking, with a pleasant open face and blue eyes. She smiled at him. 'It's all right. No harm done.'

'What a very forgiving woman.' He returned her smile. Releasing her arms, he stepped back and, head on one side, surveyed her with guileless appreciation. 'By the way, my name's David Law.'

'Luce Weston.'

'Just arrived?'

46   JOY BRINGER

'I came yesterday.'

'Holiday?'

'Work mostly.'

Having glanced at her ringless hands, he cleared his throat. 'I suppose you wouldn't care to join me for dinner tonight?'

'I'm afraid I can't.'

'Another night?' he persisted hopefully.

She smiled at him once more, liking him. 'Perhaps.'

'See you around.' He gave her a grin and took the stairs two at a time.

Luce turned her head and across the foyer met Michele Lorenzo's furious silvery-green eyes. Such a combination of fire and ice was in that one glance that unconsciously she faltered. Controlling a cowardly impulse to run the other way, she somehow moved sedately towards him.

He had risen to his feet and was waiting for her. 'A friend of yours?' he enquired.

'No.'

Meeting his eyes, their expression now cool and shuttered, Luce wondered if she had just imagined that blazing look.

'You *seemed* very friendly,' he pursued. 'In fact, I wondered if *he* might be the reason your engagement is off.'

'If that were the case I'd hardly have accepted *your* invitation,' she pointed out with some asperity.

'So how well *do* you know each other?'

'That was the first time we'd met.'

'Of course. . . I'd momentarily lost sight of what a fast worker you are.' Once again he sounded as if he was *accusing* her of something.

Rattled, her cheeks hot with resentment, she snapped, 'I don't know what you're implying, but I do know I'm fed up with your snide remarks.'

She turned on her heel to leave him standing, but he

JOY BRINGER

was too quick for her. Seizing her arm, he swung her round. 'Don't rush off.'

'Let go of me,' she spat at him.

His fingers bit in deeper, keeping her there. 'We've a date, remember?'

She shook her head. 'I've no intention of going out with you.'

'And I've no intention of letting you walk away.'

Glaring at him, she said, 'So what do you plan to do, stay here all night?'

'Not on your life. I've already been here over half an hour.'

There seemed to be an impasse until, with a sudden and complete change of attitude, he added with a grin, 'Though I must say the wait was worth it—you're looking quite delightful.'

Taking her hand, he raised it to his lips. 'Suppose we call a truce?'

Thrown into utter confusion by his volte-face, and the brush of his lips over her knuckles, she found herself agreeing, 'Very well.'

He smiled down at her. 'Now, is there anything in particular you'd like to do or see?'

His smile held such magnetism that her breath caught in her throat and her heart began to race. 'I. . .I don't mind,' she stammered. 'Oh, anything. . . Everything.'

'It seems we have a busy night ahead,' he remarked wickedly.

Determined not to let him keep the advantage, she bundled the unwanted attraction she felt for him into a cupboard and locked the door on it, before retorting sweetly, 'Well, as your invitation was so *pressing*, I thought I might as well take full advantage of it.'

A gleam in his eyes, he said, 'I hope you'll feel like that about every invitation I tender.'

Having no smart answer ready, she turned conveniently deaf.

48 JOY BRINGER

She was fast coming to terms with the fact that there were two sides to this man. His dark face usually held a cool austereness but it was a severity which, fast as quicksilver, could melt into warmth and charm. On the surface. Whether this charm was involuntary, or used deliberately as a mask to hide his real feelings, she could only guess.

'Let me take your key.'

He strolled across the foyer to deposit her room key and spoke to the middle-aged receptionist behind the desk, who straightened respectfully. Both men glanced in her direction, then the receptionist nodded.

Michele rejoined her and they set off on foot. Very conscious of her companion, of his height and his easy masculine grace, Luce concentrated on keeping a fair amount of space between them.

His sideways glance told her he'd noticed the manoeuvre but he merely smiled as if, knowing he could curtail it at any time, he was *allowing* her that small freedom.

The sun had lost its fierce heat and the air was golden and balmy. As they walked along the narrow *fondamenta* a black, steel-prowed gondola glided past.

'Did you ride in one last night?' Michele asked, following her gaze.

She shook her head and answered lightly, 'My romantic soul was disappointed. We had to make do with a water-taxi.'

When they reached St Mark's Square, with its usual motley crowd of tourists and pigeons, corn-sellers and hawkers, he paused outside Florian's and suggested, 'What about a long, cool drink?'

'Heaven,' she agreed.

Settled at a small, round, open-air table, Luce sipped a delicious fruit cocktail chinking with ice, and thought back to the previous evening when she'd sat in almost this same spot and looked so eagerly for one special face.

Becoming aware that Michele was studying her as if tuning into her thoughts, she hurriedly indicated the colourful pageant moving against the magnificent backdrop of St Mark's and the clock tower, and said, 'It's wonderful, isn't it?'

'Even more so after dark.'

She nodded. 'I was walking back from here last night when I got lost. . .'

'And imagined someone was following you.'

'I'm usually fairly level-headed,' she defended herself ruefully.

Reaching across the table, Michele took her hand, and, holding it in both of his, turned it to examine the palm. In the portentous voice of a fortune-teller he intoned, 'A beautifully shaped, capable hand, denoting a sensible, well-balanced young woman. . .'

There was nothing remotely sensible or well-balanced about the turmoil of emotions his touch was arousing, Luce thought distractedly.

'. . .except in certain circumstances,' he added in his normal crisp voice, his silvery-green eyes glinting. 'And unless the young woman in question is a fiery, imaginative Aries.'

Her smug silence told him he was wrong.

'So what *are* you?'

'What are *you*?' She refused to give an inch.

So did he. 'Guess.'

'A Leo,' she said unhesitatingly.

His white teeth gleamed. 'What makes you think that?'

'Because you're proud, arrogant, opinionated. . .'

He raised a winged brow.

'And then there's your *palazzo*.'

'Ah. . . But Ca' del Leone has been called that since the days of the doges. . . As to my sign, you've already

50 JOY BRINGER

been given an important clue. You should have no difficulty guessing if you're at all familiar with the zodiac.'

'I'm not to any great extent,' she confessed. 'It's Aunt Maureen who's interested. She would be fascinated by Peter Sebastian's sculptures. . .'

Luce paused as a thought struck her, then triumphantly she exclaimed, 'You're a Gemini, of course! Which came first, the chicken or the egg?'

Michele laughed. 'You mean, did I have the cats before the sculpture was done? I did, as a matter of fact.'

He leaned back in his chair and regarded her intently while a warm breeze which had sprung up ruffled his black hair. 'Now, let me see. . . I should say you're definitely a fire sign, with a passionate mouth to match a passionate nature. . .'

So he'd looked straight through her cool façade as if it were glass. Straight into her head.

'. . .if we rule out Aries and Leo that leaves only Sagittarius.' He smiled a little grimly. 'And do you know what that makes us?'

'Incompatible,' Luce answered, and smiled back. But all at once her heart felt as if it was crushed in ice.

She was trying to find something witty and amusing to say to dispel the gloom when, his glass now empty, Michele rose to his feet in one lithe movement. 'If you'll excuse me, I have to make a phone call.'

It was hardly likely to be business at this hour. Was he phoning Didi Lombard? Struggling with a painful emotion which she preferred not to analyse, but which felt uncomfortably like jealousy, Luce watched his tall figure disappear into the café.

How ridiculous to feel such a sense of possession, of *oneness* with a man she'd only just met. Especially when it was quite obvious he felt no reciprocal emotion.

He returned relatively quickly, looking well satisfied, and asked, 'Ready?'

She nodded, and they set off again to find a Venice few tourists saw. An enchanted place of quiet waterways and lacy bridges, of picturesque squares and little shrines, of fountains and statues and vine-shaded courtyards. A multi-faceted city that blended past and present into a glorious pageant. Luce sighed. No wonder it was termed the jewel of the Adriatic.

'Somewhat different from the Piazzale Roma,' she commented at length.

'A place to be avoided at all costs,' he agreed.

'I saw you there when I got off the airport bus.' The remark was out before she'd considered the wisdom of it.

Momentarily he looked both startled and annoyed. Then, his expression tuned to register only mild surprise, he asked, 'How on earth do you pick one person from that kind of crowd?'

Unable to say, Because I felt as if I knew you, as if I'd always known you; because your face was as familiar to me as my own, she replied weakly, 'Sometimes a particular face stands out. One of the important things we learnt at art college was how to note and store detail.'

'I see, a trained eye.' For a second or two he said nothing further, then, apparently going along with her unspoken wish to change the subject, he asked, tongue in cheek, 'And what did you think of our transport?'

'It was like the black hole of Calcutta on wheels. I struggled off an absolute wreck.'

He shook his head with spurious sympathy. 'I'm sorry, I should have asked Signor Candiano to warn you that the buses get a little crowded.'

Luce was well aware that beneath his bland expression he was highly entertained, and for a moment she felt aggrieved. But, determined that he shouldn't have the satisfaction of seeing her vexation, she said drily, 'Don't mention it; I'm only glad it wasn't rush-hour.'

He laughed, his excellent teeth a gleaming flash of white against his tan. 'Wonder of wonders! A woman with a sense of humour.'

'That's a very chauvinistic remark, and only goes to prove you must be associating with the wrong kind of woman.' The retort was out before she could prevent it.

He gave her a sharp look, but said nothing.

Twilight had crept out of hiding and was stealthily wrapping the dying day in lavender shrouds, before they stopped at a small *trattoria* alongside one of the quieter canals.

Luigi, the fat, jovial owner, greeted Michele like an old friend. Having waved them to a table, he flourished two wine glasses, which he filled to the brim with an excellent Chianti, before heading for the kitchen.

'Earlier you mentioned college,' Michele remarked. 'How long were you there?'

It was an innocuous question, so why did she suddenly feel as if she were facing the Inquisition?

Swallowing, she answered, 'Only two years. I had intended to go on and become a teacher, but when Dad died of a heart attack I was needed to help run the family art gallery.'

'Haven't you any brothers or sisters?'

'No, I'm an only child.'

'You mentioned an Aunt Maureen.'

'My father's sister. She's running the gallery at the moment, with the help of a young assistant.'

'Has she a family?'

'No. She hasn't married. She says she's still waiting for the right man.'

'What about your mother?'

Luce swallowed. 'She was killed last year. A road

JOY BRINGER

accident.' Still unable to discuss her mother's death without the risk of tears, she said abruptly, 'Tell me about Venice.'

'Past or present?' he queried.

'Past. How long have your family lived here?'

'For hundreds of years. My ancestors were wealthy and powerful; they owned a vast amount of property and a fleet of merchant ships.

'In the sixteenth century my namesake was made a doge. He was a brilliant man who had a great deal of influence—in fact, he was one of the few doges who wielded any real authority.

'His strength, courage, and wisdom were legendary. Part of the crest on his ducal coat of arms was a lion, and he became known as the Lion of Venice. That, of course, is where the *palazzo* got its name. . .'

Sitting in the warm purply-blue dusk, watching an ethereal moon rise, trailing diaphanous veils of cloud, they ate a leisurely meal of iced cucumber soup, lasagne, *dolcelatte*, and tangy apricots.

'That was delicious,' Luce remarked with a sigh of contentment.

'I'm pleased to see you've an appetite,' Michele observed.

Ruefully she admitted, 'I'm always hungry,' and thought how very unromantic that sounded.

'You're so slim that I thought you might be one of those women who are on a perpetual diet, and I dislike intensely dining with someone who eats like a sparrow.'

She compounded it. 'I'm more the vulture variety.'

All at once she had the uncomfortable feeling that he had found some deeper meaning in her remark and was silently agreeing with her; then he laughed, and the moment passed.

When Luigi carried out a tray of coffee and liqueurs Michele asked him something in a low tone. The fat man beamed and nodded happily before hurrying away.

JOY BRINGER

While Luce added a liberal amount of sugar and cream to her coffee a question that had been submerged in her mind suddenly resurfaced, and she queried, 'How did you know where I was staying?'

'I beg your pardon?'

'You didn't ask, and I didn't tell you, so how did you know which hotel to take me to?'

Just for a moment Michele looked disconcerted, then said easily, 'Signor Candiano must have mentioned it when I saw him this afternoon.'

Had the agent known? Luce couldn't recall referring to the Trevi by name. . . Still, she must have done.

When they'd finished their second cup of coffee her companion murmured, 'Time for one more thing.' He rose and held out his hand.

Of its own volition hers went into it like a homing pigeon while her mind was still saying, 'No way, *signore.*'

As he drew her to the canal's edge a gondola slid from out of the shadows.

'A waterborne chariot to please your romantic soul,' he said with lazy mockery.

Feeling embarrassed now, Luce drew back, trying to free her hand. 'I was only joking when I——'

He put a finger to her lips, making her heart slam against her ribs. 'Don't let Luigi hear you say that; he'll be very disappointed. *He* has a romantic soul, and he was delighted to think he might be playing Cupid.'

So the fat proprietor had whistled up the gondola. Well, he'd just have to be disappointed. . .

But Michele was urging her down the steps, and the gondolier had reached up to assist her into the gently rocking craft.

With something less than her usual grace she sat down in the stern, then tensed as Michele lowered his lean body into the space beside her, his arm stretched

JOY BRINGER

casually along the back of the ornate black wooden seat.

For a while Luce sat mutely as the gondolier, dressed for the part in a red and white striped shirt and a straw hat with a red ribbon, plied his single oar. Then, anxious to find something to say, she remarked inanely, 'Thank you. It's been a nice evening.'

'Nice!' Michele echoed caustically. 'There's no need to be so schoolgirlishly polite.'

'There's no need to be so insufferably rude,' she countered angrily.

'I'm sorry.' His apology was immediate.

It was followed by a silence so fraught with regret on Luce's part that after a few seconds she had to admit the truth. 'It was my fault. Nice is a lukewarm word. Almost any other adjective would have been more appropriate.' Like exciting, thrilling, disturbing, magical. . .

'You're a very exceptional woman,' Michele said slowly. 'I've never met one quite like you before. There are times when you leave me speechless.'

'Now *that* I doubt.'

His smile deepening, he reached out and touched her cheek in a light caress. 'Did I apologise?'

'You did.' She was proud of the fact that her voice was steady.

'Adequately?' His eyes were on her mouth.

'Quite adequately,' she assured him hastily, and, moving as far away as the seat would allow, looked straight ahead, her spine stiff, her shoulders squared.

After a while the gentle rocking as they moved smoothly over the dark water, the beauty and romance of the night, began to work a subtle magic, and unconsciously she relaxed.

'That's better,' Michele's amused voice said in her ear. 'I wondered why you felt the need to act like some outraged maiden aunt.'

'I was doing nothing of the kind,' she denied crossly, turning to face him.

It was a mistake. The move brought his mouth much too close to hers, and he took advantage of that fact before she had time to even consider evasive action.

His kiss was as sensuous and seductive as black satin, sweeter than any wine. When she should have been indignantly pulling away somehow she was melting into his arms, her lips parting beneath the increasing ardour of his.

It was as satisfying as coming home, lovely as a May morning, exhilarating as a roller-coaster ride, fierce as a forest fire, and she never wanted it to end. . . Until, like a jet of cold water, she remembered Didi Lombard's words; ". . .you'd get on better by being nice to the girl. . .you could have her eating out of your hand."

Luce checked her first impulse, which had been to tear herself free. Wouldn't it take the wind out of his sails more thoroughly if she seemed *indifferent* rather than angry?

Though still apparently co-operating, she forced herself to switch off completely.

He sensed the change at once and lifted his dark head.

She could tell that he was puzzled, and not a little put out. Piling the agony on, she said cheerfully, 'Well, now we've got *that* out of the way. . .'

'*What* out of the way?'

'The mandatory love-scene,' she explained, as though talking to a half-wit.

'Why, you little. . .!' Briefly he looked outraged, then, throwing back his head, he burst out laughing.

He had a nice laugh, deep and musical and infectious.

After a moment or two he stopped laughing, and, in the fitful light of a moon playing hide and seek behind its veils of cloud, searched her face. He was so close

JOY BRINGER

that his breath stirred a tendril of hair loose against her cheek. 'So what made you do it?'

She felt as if she was drowning. 'Do what?'

An edge of barely concealed displeasure to his tone, he answered, 'Turn our romantic little episode into a farce.'

A romantic little episode, yet the intensity of what she'd felt in those moments could have overwhelmed her completely if she hadn't remembered Didi's words. And she could have sworn that, after the first second or two, he had been caught up by the same strong feeling. A feeling he now seemed annoyed about, eager to negate.

'You were warm and willing in my arms, then all at once. . .' His eyes narrowed dangerously.

Luce surfaced and took a deep breath. 'I'm sorry if I've bruised your ego, if you're angry. . .'

Cupping her chin, he brushed the pad of his thumb across her lips. 'Oh, no, *cara*,' he denied softly, 'I'm not angry.' His hand slid down to rest lightly against her throat. 'I always abide by the old saying, "Don't get mad, get even." '

Shivers running through her, she said with as much insouciance as she could muster, 'I'm very tired, and it's work tomorrow. Do you think we could get back?'

Removing his hand, he told her equably, 'We're practically there.'

Almost giddy with nervous tension and a feeling she refused to acknowledge as *fear*, Luce sighed with relief. She hadn't realised that they were so close. At night everything looked different, the smaller canals were like a labyrinth, and apart from an occasional lamp it was quite dark when the moon was hidden.

Proving the truth of his words, after a few hundred yards the gondola drew alongside some steps. Eager for the haven of her hotel room, Luce allowed Michele to help her on to the deserted *fondamenta*. Only when he

58   JOY BRINGER

stooped and some lire changed hands did she realise
that he must be intending to walk back.

As the gondolier dipped his oar and the graceful craft
slid silently away she peered about her. All she could
see in the gloom was the high stone wall of some
building. Her heart-rate suddenly quickening, Luce
objected, 'I don't recognise this at all. Where are we?'

Taking a key from his pocket, Michele unlocked a
metal-studded door set in the wall before answering
with soft satisfaction, 'At the south entrance to the Ca'
del Leone. I decided to come this way because I wanted
you to see the courtyard by moonlight.'

She drew back. He might just as well have enticed,
"Won't you walk into my parlour?"

Picking up her thoughts as if she'd broadcast them,
he added mockingly, 'There is no winding stair and I
promise not to eat you. So do come inside.'

Deliberately rude and prosaic, she said, 'Thank you,
but I'm much too tired to bother looking at courtyards.
All I want is to get to bed as soon as possible.'

'Well, if that's what you want, who am I to argue?'
He opened the door into a kind of vaulted tunnel lit by
overhead lamps, and indicated that she should precede
him.

Heart beating even faster, she shook her head. 'I've
no intention of coming into the *palazzo* at this time of
night.'

'You just expressed a somewhat urgent desire to go
to bed.'

'My *own* bed,' she said stiffly. 'And that's back at the
hotel.'

'I'm afraid you're wrong.' He managed to sound
apologetic.

'What do you mean, I'm wrong?' Her voice was
shrill, the alarm undisguised now.

'Come inside and I'll explain.' He went through the

door and waited quietly, confidently, showing no sign of impatience.

Luce glanced along the *fondamenta*. There was no one in sight and the canal was deserted, the water slopping gently like a cup of black coffee in an unsteady hand.

'This area is private,' he told her. 'No boats come past here. And at both ends of the quay iron railings run right to the canal's edge.'

The moon had come out again—even the moon did as he wanted, she thought hopelessly—and across the water she could see only high walls and shuttered windows.

Yet the Grand Canal must be quite close. It would have boats on it, lights and music, and people still thronging the bars and restaurants. It represented safety.

But it might as well have been a million miles away.

Shoulders back, head held high, she stepped past him, going to meet danger—and she had no doubt that it *was* danger—with an answering surge of excitement.

CHAPTER FOUR

HAVING the door locked behind her, as though she'd entered a prison, sent a prickle of nameless apprehension down Luce's spine. Don't be a fool, she scolded herself silently as Michele led the way down the echoing tunnel to a fancy wrought-iron gate at the far end.

The gate opened into a magnificent courtyard paved with huge slabs of stone, an enchanted place of moonlit trees and silvered statuary. The courtyard of the Beast's castle, Luce decided fancifully, with all his courtiers turned to marble.

She gazed around her, impressed in spite of her unease and her determination to appear indifferent. Ca' del Leone was built in a rectangle, its long inner windows and doors opening on to a grand terrace surrounding the courtyard.

His hand beneath her elbow, Michele directed her down a short flight of steps to a central sunken garden where Neptune, brandishing a trident, guarded a splashing fountain.

On all sides were banks of flowers, and climbing shrubs and vines formed a partial canopy to keep out the fierce sun. It must have been most pleasant by day. At night it was magical.

He indicated a swing-seat, but with a shake of her head she refused to sit, preferring to stand and go straight into the attack. 'Do you always have to use this much persuasion to show off the courtyard?'

Smiling mirthlessly, he admitted, 'Despite your romantic soul, you are my most reluctant guest so far.'

'I haven't got a romantic soul.'

'Of course you have.'

60

JOY BRINGER

'You don't know anything about me.'

'But I know a great deal about you. Though in some ways you differ, you have typical Sagittarian flair and warmth, the ability to act, to play the clown, perhaps to hide a more serious side, the willingness to gamble. . .'

They were standing in deep shadow but she saw the gleam of his teeth. 'At this moment you'd like to take a gamble and be transported into a world of sensual delight. But you're scared stiff, and I can't help but wonder why.'

He was much too close and she could hear his heartbeat. Or was it her own?

'I am not scared,' she said belligerently. 'I'm just tired and cross at being coerced like this when all I want to do is——'

'Go to bed,' he finished for her. Adding, 'Do you know, I'm beginning to find this unashamed eagerness to get to bed intriguing, to say the least?'

Refusing to rise to the bait, she visualised and counted ten elephants, a hangover habit from her childhood, then, her voice tightly controlled, asked, 'Would you please explain why you insisted on bringing me here instead of taking me to the Trevi?'

'There was no point in going back to the hotel. You no longer have a room there.' As she gaped at him he went on calmly, 'I told them you would be staying at the *palazzo* and asked them to have your luggage repacked and sent over here.'

'I don't believe they would do such a thing without my permission.'

But even as she spoke she recalled his handing in her key and speaking to the clerk, then both of them looking across at her. Oh, but he was clever, and with that air of authority, that assurance, who would dream of arguing with him?

As if reading her thoughts, he smiled.

62 JOY BRINGER

'And the phone call you made?' she asked, knowing the answer.

'To make sure a room was prepared for you.'

It went against the grain to let him win. But at the height of the tourist season it was odds on that her old room had already been taken, and she couldn't see herself tramping Venice at this time of night, looking for alternative accommodation. In any case, he had her belongings.

'You had no right to alter my arrangements without consulting me,' she said tightly.

'When we have so many spare rooms here it seemed eminently sensible, much better than allowing you to travel backwards and forwards.'

Although it *sounded* convincing, she was oddly certain that the travelling had very little to do with it. Recalling his reaction after she'd bumped into David Law, she felt sure that at least part of the reason was to have her under his eye. *Under surveillance.* A chill ran through her.

She was very tempted to ask just what was going on. But if he *was* playing some bizarre game he was hardly likely to admit it.

Or was she being melodramatic? Sagittarians, Aunt Maureen was fond of telling her, had a strong sense of theatre and tended to exaggerate situations and emotions. Perhaps she was reading too much into——

'Are they for sale?' His voice broke into her abstraction.

'I was only thinking that if you're always so high-handed in your dealings with people it's a wonder you haven't had your come-uppance.'

He said ironically, 'I thought I had, earlier. And, though I have my suspicions as to the cause, I'd like to *know* what made you act the way you did.'

A sudden reckless urge to play with fire made her

deliberately provoke him. 'You can't credit that I just got bored?'

She heard the breath hiss through his teeth. Then one arm was clamping her to him, and his free hand was forcing up her chin.

His kiss was an assault, punitive, compelling her lips to part, robbing her of breath. Nothing like this had ever happened to her before, and she should have been afraid.

But somehow she wasn't. Her entire being thrown into wild, sweet confusion, she met fire with fire, passion with passion. This man was hers, as she was his; they were two halves of a whole.

He was kissing her now with a delicate urgency, her cheeks and temples, her closed eyelids and long, slender throat. Arms wound around his neck, she shivered while his hands moved over her slim body, tracing her curves through the flimsy material of her dress, leaving a singing excitement in their wake.

Filled with a *need*, a *hunger* that was as much spiritual as bodily, she wanted them to meet on every level, be one in every sense of the word.

When abruptly he lifted his head and set her from him, dazed and disorientated, she staggered a little before regaining her balance.

'You have a novel way of showing boredom,' he drawled.

But even in her bemused state she heard, with fierce satisfaction, the harshness, the rapid breathing that belied his attempt to sound unmoved.

Aching for him, longing to be back in his arms, she whispered, 'Michele. . .I'm sorry I. . .'

But he was turning away, saying flatly, 'It's very late. I'd better show you your room.'

Don't get mad, get even, she thought, and knew he was doing just that.

Stumbling a little, she followed him up the steps and

64 JOY BRINGER

across the moonlit terrace into the *palazzo*. Wall sconces providing a dim light, they climbed the staircase in silence.

Part-way along a wide marble corridor he stopped and indicated one of the many elaborately carved doors. 'This is your room.'

Chilled and oppressed by the emptiness, the echoing vastness, she glanced around uncertainly.

Walking into her mind with his usual ease, he said brusquely, 'It's all right. You won't need to leave it.'

'I'm glad about that.' She tried to sound airy. 'I might never find it again—these doors all look alike.'

'Not really.' With a lean finger he indicated an unusual mask-like carving on the centre panel, showing two identical faces looking in opposite directions. 'This is Janus, the god of doors. As you can see, he has two faces, not because *he* was deceitful, but because every door looks two ways.'

While Luce wondered if she'd only imagined that emphasis on the *he* Michele went on, 'I chose this room especially for you.' There was a brittleness to his tone. '*Buona notte*.'

He strolled to the door opposite and, his hand on the knob, turned to look at her. His gaze moved from her startled face down the length of her body and lingered on her slim bare legs. Casually he remarked, 'There's a spider crawling up your leg.'

Luce jumped and brushed frantically at her legs. Since childhood she'd had a quite irrational dread of spiders.

Smiling grimly, he closed the door behind him.

It was several seconds before it dawned on her that his last words had been spoken in Italian.

Her room was large and comfortable, with pale walls, light, modern furniture and an *en suite* bathroom. Having investigated, she found that her luggage had been unpacked, her night-wear and toilet things put in

JOY BRINGER

65

their appropriate places, and her clothes hung neatly in the walk-in wardrobe. Her undies and the sandalwood box were in the top drawer of the dressing-table.

An electric kettle and all the paraphernalia for making tea and coffee stood on a bedside table alongside a biscuit-barrel and bowl of cream roses.

It seemed as if he'd thought of everything.

He was a clever, devious swine, she reflected bitterly as she cleaned her teeth and prepared for bed. All that talk about Janus, just to let her know he'd suspected her of lying. *And finally caught her out.*

Normally lies and deceit were anathema to her, and she was angry and rueful that since meeting him she had *twice* allowed circumstances to trap her into using them.

Guiltily she wished she'd admitted to her previous engagement. It had been a silly, spur-of-the-moment impulse to deny it, but by lying to him she'd put herself in an invidious position.

Then she'd added to her sins by trying to hide the fact that she spoke Italian.

Still, it was no big deal, she tried to soothe her conscience. No one had been hurt. Except herself. And that hurt was slight, compared to what it might have been if things hadn't happened the way they had tonight.

Luce sighed. Although forewarned that he was deliberately "being nice" to her, she could, totally out of character, have counted the world well lost and ended up in his bed if he himself hadn't called a halt by way of retaliation.

Even now the magnetism that drew her to him was so strong that if he knocked at her door and said he'd changed his mind, in spite of everything, it might take more *amor proprio* than she could muster to refuse him.

Shame on you! she scolded herself, banking down

66 .JOY BRINGER

the passion, trying for a lighter note. A well-brought-up young lady and a virgin to boot shouldn't be having such thoughts.

Especially when her *innamorato* was a man she knew virtually nothing about. A man whose actions and motives she had plenty of cause to doubt. *A man whose star sign made him her exact opposite*.

Though impulsive in some ways, she was an ordinary, practical girl who had never really believed in grand passion or love at first sight. She had always felt that liking should come first then gradually deepen into love.

Now, unsure about liking him, convinced that they were incompatible, she knew she loved him. It had happened in a split-second. But what did time signify? How long did it take lightning to strike? And once it had struck its effects were irreversible.

If, a week ago, someone had told her it might happen to her she would have laughed and treated it as a huge joke. Only now that it had happened it wasn't in the least funny.

Climbing into bed, she switched out the light and turned on to her side. With so much on her mind and her emotions still in a turmoil she didn't expect to sleep but, a hand beneath her cheek, she was fast off within seconds.

Luce was awakened by a tapping. Opening her eyes, she peered into the gloom. Momentarily her mind was a confused blank, then, like taking a lens cap from a camera, everything came into clear mental focus.

Struggling into a sitting position, she peered at her watch, then called, 'Come in.'

The door opened to admit Rosa, wearing her customary black.

'*Buon giorno, signorina.*'

'*Buon giorno, Rosa,*' Luce replied.

Carefully the housekeeper placed the tray she was

JOY BRINGER

carrying across Luce's knees, before opening the shutters and flooding the room with light.

Blinking, Luce asked, 'Can you tell me what time it is, Rosa? I'm afraid my watch has stopped.'

'It is nine-thirty, *signorina*. . . Signor Diomede said to give you his compliments and tell you to take the morning off. He himself will be out until lunchtime'.

Luce frowned. 'Signor Diomede?'

'*Si.*'

Rosa had reached the door when Luce asked, 'Who is Signor Diomede?'

Her dark eyes puzzled, the housekeeper answered, 'Why, the *padrone di casa, signorina.*'

For a few seconds Luce sat staring at the closed door, trying to make sense of this latest development, before looking down at the tray.

It was set with a full English breakfast—well, she had told Michele she was always hungry—and while she poured herself some coffee and began on the bacon and eggs she recalled their first meeting. When she had asked his name there had been a slight, but noticeable, hesitation before he'd answered.

She sighed. Yet another loose piece in the puzzle. If only she could fit the jigsaw together and get a clear picture of this man who so intrigued her. But he seemed to *want* to be a man of mystery, *want* to bamboozle her.

The question was, *why*?

Perhaps it was simply due to his star sign. He was a Gemini. A man with two faces, a man of secrets, changeable and versatile, clever and complex.

Or there might be more to it than that.

Luce shivered suddenly. Quite a few odd things had happened in the last two days and, though this was the first time she'd admitted it even to herself, she'd felt vaguely uneasy, *threatened*, ever since she'd arrived in Venice.

It might be wisest to make her apologies and go

68 JOY BRINGER

home. If she broke free now, before the silken bonds that bound her to Michele had a chance to grow any tighter, she might save herself untold heartache, if nothing else.

But even as the thought took shape she dismissed it. It was already too late. She could no more walk away from him now than she could voluntarily stop breathing.

So she would stay and see what the future brought. After all, she told herself boldly, an element of risk, of danger, added a certain amount of spice to life.

Her breakfast finished, she showered and dressed in a beige and white skirt and plain beige top and, after a slight struggle with the clasp, fastened her gold locket around her neck before setting off to explore. Once she could find her way around the *palazzo* she wouldn't feel quite so helpless.

After wandering about for a while she finally got her bearings and found the splendid staircase that led to the grand hall and the main entrance. From there she made her way to Michele's office and tapped on the door.

Didi Lombard's voice called, 'Come in.'

Luce obeyed.

'Ah, Miss Weston, I thought it might be you.' Didi, attractive in a lime-green dress and jacket, smiled charmingly. 'I hope you slept well?'

'Very well, thank you.' Luce stooped to stroke Poll, who was winding silently and sinuously round her ankles.

Didi regarded the cat without favour. 'Michele lets those wretched animals have the run of the place. God knows why. Personally I wish he'd left them to drown.'

'Left them to drown?'

Hearing the outrage in Luce's voice, Didi spread both hands in a dismissive gesture. 'Venice is full of unwanted cats. They were only tiny kittens. Someone had put them in a box and thrown them into the canal.

JOY BRINGER

Michele spotted it when it was just about to sink and was fool enough to go in fully clothed.'

'I think that was marvellous of him,' Luce cried hotly.

Didi shrugged, then in her usual pleasant manner said, 'I was just on my way out. Is there anything I can do for you before I go?'

Resisting the temptation to ask for answers to some of the questions that had been plaguing her, Luce shook her head. 'Not really. But I would like to ring London, if that's all right?'

'Feel free.' Didi indicated the phone on the desk. 'I'm sure Michele would want you to treat the *palazzo* as home. Bye, then.'

Luce dialled the international code and the Piccadilly number. There were several clicks, then Maureen said, 'Ventura Gallery.'

Only when she heard her aunt's familiar voice and had to fight a desire to burst into tears did Luce realise just how strung-up she'd been.

'I was wondering when you'd ring.' Maureen sounded chirpy. 'How are things going?'

'Fine,' Luce replied tritely and without a great deal of truth. There was so much to say, and if they'd been face to face she would have poured it all out, but as it was. . .'I'm not at the hotel any longer. I'm staying at the Ca' del Leone, a *palazzo* on the Grand Canal.'

'Sounds posh.'

'It is.'

'Signor Candiano's?' Maureen hazarded.

'No. A man named Michele. . .' Luce hesitated briefly '. . .Diomede owns it.'

'So who is this Michele Diomede? How does he fit in?'

'I'm not sure,' Luce admitted, fingering her locket. 'He's a friend of Peter Sebastian's, I gather, and he seems to be running things.'

'What's he like?'

'Tall, dark and handsome. A hackneyed phrase but a true description,' Luce answered flippantly.

'Married?'

'Apparently not. Why do you ask?'

'Because I should say he has a powerful effect on you. Your voice changes when you talk about him.'

Shaken by her aunt's shrewdness, Luce said nothing.

'By the way, have you rung Paul yet?' Maureen demanded.

'No, I. . .'

'Well, I suggest you do. He's grumpy because he hasn't heard from you.'

'I don't know what to say to him,' Luce confessed. Then in a rush, 'I've decided the engagement was a bad mistake. I don't want to tell him over the phone, but at the same time I can't pretend everything's all right.'

'I think you should let him know where he stands,' Maureen said. 'You can't leave him in ignorance for weeks. It's not fair to him. And, until you've told him, *you* won't feel free.' Craftily she added, 'It might cramp your style where this Michele Diomede is concerned.'

If only you knew! Luce thought, suddenly ashamed that in Michele's arms she hadn't even remembered Paul's existence.

'Do you happen to know his star sign?' Maureen asked.

'What?'

'Michele Diomede's star sign. . .?'

'I do, as a matter of fact.' Luce tried to speak casually. 'He's a Gemini.'

'Is he, now?'

Please don't tell me we're totally wrong for each other, Luce begged silently, I already know.

But Maureen was saying hastily, 'Liz isn't in today, and I've got what appears to be a customer, so I'd better go. Keep in touch, won't you? Bye, love.'

JOY BRINGER 71

Just before the line went dead a sharp click sounded as an extension was replaced. Someone had undoubtedly been listening, and been caught by the abrupt ending to the conversation.

But who? Michele wasn't in, and Didi had gone out. Or had she? It was hardly likely that any of the servants would have listened.

Feeling restless and on edge, Luce decided to go into the garden. She would have opted to work, only she had no idea what Michele had done with the key to the studio door.

She was endeavouring to find her way to the courtyard when, reaching the end of one of the wide corridors, she found herself in a long gallery lined with portraits.

As she stood on the crimson carpet, hesitating, the chandeliers suddenly flashed on, dispelling the gloom. Turning, she found Michele almost at her elbow. His dark face wore the cool, slightly ironic expression that she was getting to know well.

Her heart tumbling about like a circus clown, and suddenly breathless, she said, 'I thought you were out.'

'I was, but as you can see I returned a little early.' He indicated the paintings, and asked, 'Were you about to view my ancestors, Luce?'

'No, I was trying to find my way into the garden.'

He took her elbow. 'Then allow me to show you.'

Looking anywhere but at him, she submitted, trying to control the feverish excitement his touch always aroused.

Outside, in the open air, it was glorious. A great yellow sun like a runaway balloon shone from a deep blue sky, and a cooling breeze from the lagoon mitigated the heat.

When they reached the sunken garden, ignoring the swing-seat beneath the vines, Luce chose a sunny bench and, battening down her agitation, prepared for battle.

'You should keep in the shade,' Michele advised. 'Venetian sun can be very deceptive, and with such a delicate skin——'

'I love the sun,' Luce interrupted firmly, 'and I never burn.' Politely she added, 'But thank you for your concern, Signor Diomede.'

Taking a seat by her side, he said, 'So now you know who I am.' It sounded like a challenge, a gauntlet thrown down.

For the first time she risked a glance at that dark Renaissance face with its clear-cut features and winged brows, the beautiful, thickly lashed eyes and chiselled mouth, the cleft chin and strong jaw. 'Why did you say your name was Michele Lorenzo?'

'Because it is. Michele Lorenzo Diomede. I thought you might have guessed.' His voice was indolent, but his brilliant eyes watched her with an intensity that belied that lazy unconcern.

'If this is some kind of guessing game you'll have to count me out. I haven't got an intricate mind. I've always been hopeless at riddles. I can't even solve crosswords,' she added for good measure.

His shoulders moved in a slight shrug. 'Yet you can be devious enough.'

He'd spoken the last words in Italian, and in Italian as fluent and colloquial as his own she answered, 'I'm sorry about that. It isn't my usual style, but I thought it would be less embarrassing if I——'

'There's no need to explain,' he said smoothly, reverting to English. 'I quite understand.'

Taking her chin between his thumb and forefinger, he held her face so that he could scrutinise it. 'What I *don't* understand is why you appear to blame me for something *someone else* thought and said.'

He was quite right, she *had* blamed him. 'I. . .I'm sorry. . .' She faltered to a halt.

JOY BRINGER

His fingers tightened, while silvery-green eyes looked deep into gold.

'Perhaps we could ignore what is past and start again?' he suggested.

She nodded, all her doubts dispelled as night's shadows were dispelled by the light of day. Gladness filled her, irradiating her whole face, making her eyes glow.

'You're quite lovely,' he said softly. 'I can see how easily you'd bewitch any man.'

Was she just imagining an underlying bitterness in his remark? Before she could be sure his mouth covered hers, banishing thought, leaving nothing but feeling. Her whole being was centred on him, wrapped up in him.

His kiss was pure joy, winging happiness, as if her spirit was soaring into a clear sky.

She floated down to earth slowly, to find him studying her dazed face with an unmistakable gleam of triumph in his eyes.

'Don't overestimate your. . .effect on me,' she muttered in an attempt to salvage some pride.

He smiled. 'Don't underestimate the effect we have on each other. At a more appropriate time I will be happy to prove to you just how much excitement and delight our mutual attraction can generate.'

Mutual attraction.

Though 'attraction' was an anaemic description of *her* feelings, still she hugged the words to her like some priceless gift. He did, albeit reluctantly, feel *something* positive for her.

In the silence that followed the outside world gradually reasserted itself. Luce felt the sun warm on her bare arms, watched a fat, furry bee bumble among the flowers, smelt the scent of roses, and heard, as a background hum, the myriad sounds of Venice.

But part of her mind stayed with Michele. Enslaved.

Enchanted. Held in thrall. While her body, like a desert longing for rain to bring it to life, switched to hold and waited for him to fulfil his promise of delight.

What strange chemistry turned her blood to rivers of fire under this man's lightest touch, while the most passionate kisses from another had left her largely indifferent, unresponsive?

With all his good looks, his concentrated effort to win her, Paul had never affected her like this, never made her feel a fraction of what she felt now.

All at once guilt fluttered and began to beat in her mind like dark wings. Poor Paul, still in his fool's paradise.

'Aunt Maureen's right.' Unconsciously Luce spoke the thought aloud.

Michele gave her a swift, questioning glance.

A little awkwardly she explained, 'I was going to wait until I got home to tell Paul that our engagement was a mistake. But Aunt Maureen thinks I should tell him straight away.'

Some strong emotion seemed to cloud Michele's eyes, but he asked lightly enough, 'Do you and your aunt have ESP?'

'I phoned her this morning.' Luce almost added that someone had eavesdropped, but held back the accusation. After all, what did it matter really? There were no state secrets involved. She hadn't admitted feeling anything special for Michele. . .

'You haven't called your fiancé?'

She shook her head. 'I didn't know what to say to him. I. . .I'll have to write. I only wish I'd never accepted his ring. . . Oh, lord!'

'What's wrong?'

'Paul's ring. I left it in the hotel's safe.'

'That isn't a problem. We'll pick it up after lunch and it can be transferred to my office safe.' Michele rose to his feet. 'You just have time before we go to write that

JOY. BRINGER

letter.' His voice deepened, roughened. 'I want you to be free before I make love to you, not morally tied to another man.'

Later she would know a heady excitement when she thought of his words. But at that minute, having allowed them free rein, guilt and self-condemnation were riding her hard.

In her heart of hearts she had blamed Paul for his unrelenting pressure, but it was her own weakness, her failure to stand up to him, that was responsible for the situation. Now, though she *hated* hurting him, it had to be done.

Once the difficult letter was written and posted, a weight seemed to lift from her, and Luce felt almost light-hearted as Michele and she ate a tasty lunch at a small *trattoria*.

Afterwards he took her to pick up the ring. With it safely in his pocket, they were leaving the foyer, Luce leading the way, when a voice cried, 'Well, hello! I've been hoping to catch a glimpse of you.'

'Hello.' Luce smiled at David Law, and held out her hand.

He took it eagerly and, still holding it, asked, 'What about dinner tonight?'

'Miss Weston is dining with me.' Though the words were softly spoken and polite, the look in Michele's eyes made David drop her hand as if it were red-hot and step back.

His fair face going crimson, he stammered, 'I. . .I'm sorry, I didn't realise you were with. . . Perhaps another time?'

As Michele moved forward with panther-like grace David said hurriedly, 'Well I must be off—er—see you around.'

Speechless at Michele's intervention, Luce watched David's hasty retreat. She might have been amused if she hadn't been so annoyed.

76   JOY BRINGER

'A good trick,' she said sharply. 'What do you do for
an encore? Make him disappear in a puff of smoke?'

Michele looked at her sardonically. 'I'm pleased to
find that your sense of humour is still intact, even if it
does seem to be a shade cynical. As for an
encore. . . guess.' He leaned towards her, his eyes on
her mouth.

Sudden panic made her pull back. Then she gritted
her teeth. Of course he wouldn't kiss her here in a
crowded hotel foyer. He was goading her, waiting for
just that reaction.

She glanced up, met those extraordinary eyes, and
saw from the mockery in them that she'd been right.
Without another word she turned and stalked out,
leaving him to follow.

Whistling under his breath, he helped her into the
motor-boat and jumped down lightly after her. In a
moment or two they had left the Trevi behind them.

Venice, as usual, was *en fête*. A freshening breeze
broke the surface of the water into a million fragments
of dancing light and set the flags and pennants and
striped awnings fluttering gaily.

Camera-toting tourists thronged the canals and
fondas, boats bumped and jostled, and booths selling
luscious red water-melon, fizzy canned drinks, and
brightly coloured ice-cream did a roaring trade.

Sights and sounds mingled. Drifting from an open
window came the voice of a tenor singing 'O Sole Mio',
while out in the lagoon a ship's siren sounded, and on
one of the bridges a man played an accordion.

As Luce looked around her, enjoying the colourful
scene, Michele asked, 'Where would you like to go
now?'

Not without some reluctance she said, 'Back to the
palazzo. I must get some work done.'

He smiled at her with lazy charm. 'I was thinking of
taking the afternoon off.'

She resisted the impulse to be a lotus-eater. 'Well, I wasn't,' she stated firmly. 'I'm here to do a job.'

A flicker of surprise in his silvery-green eyes, Michele said, 'I'm sure Signor Candiano won't mind.'

'It isn't Signor Candiano who's paying me,' she pointed out, 'it's Peter Sebastian.'

'I'm sure *he* won't mind.' There was something in the way he spoke that riveted her attention.

'Well, as I can't ask him. . .' She broke off, a sudden wild suspicion widening her eyes, scattering her wits like a shotgun blast would scatter a flock of starlings.

After studying her face, Michele waited quietly.

'You said Peter Sebastian was in the States.' Her voice was surprisingly level.

'No, *you* said you understood he was. I didn't correct you.'

Luce dragged air into her lungs like a swimmer who had been underwater too long. 'So *Peter Sebastian* is an alias?'

'Not exactly. My full name is Michele Lorenzo Pietro Sebastiano Diomede. Quite a mouthful.'

A jeer in her voice, she said, 'No one can deny it has a ring to it.'

'That's what one does to necks,' he told her with mock menace.

When she failed to retort he cocked an eyebrow at her, waiting for the sparring to continue.

But, her mind feeling jarred, incapable of coherent thought, she sat perfectly still, staring at the planking in the bottom of the boat.

'It seems to have come as a shock to you,' he observed.

She lifted her head and looked him in the face. 'Somehow you don't look like an internationally famous sculptor.'

'I don't regard myself as such. First and foremost, I'm a businessman, the owner of several European

galleries. Sculpting has always been more of a hobby.'
He sounded casual, unconcerned.

Fury and bitterness mingled inside her. 'Why didn't
you admit who you were?' she cried. 'Why this elaborate charade?'

'I'm not the only one who goes in for charades,' he
said harshly. 'But, to answer your question, call it self-preservation.

'The last time I was in England I was foolish enough
to take a woman into my confidence. She blabbed to
the Press and they hounded me until I left the country.
Here, on my home ground, I can't afford to make that
kind of mistake.'

'I wouldn't have told anyone, believe me.'

'I do. That's why you know now.'

He steered the small boat through a jumble of
miscellaneous craft, then, with what seemed to be a
deliberate attempt to lighten the atmosphere, said, 'So
go ahead and ask me.'

'Ask you what?'

'If I mind you taking the afternoon off.'

She shook her head. 'I'd rather not, thank you. I
want to get some work done.'

There was no way she could treat this new revelation
lightly. She needed to be on her own. Have time to
think.

'Very well.' He accepted her decision. 'Then I suggest we go the Ca' del Serpente and take a look at the
possible rooms.' With a sidelong glance he added, 'If
that's all right by you?'

'Fine.' It wasn't what she'd intended, but if he was
expecting her to quibble. . .well, she refused to gratify
him.

CHAPTER FIVE

LUCE sat silent and withdrawn as they threaded their way through the busy canals. For several years she had been almost obsessed by Peter Sebastian, not only by his work, she finally admitted, but by the man himself. Perhaps she'd been a little in love with him, or at least his *image*.

From the small amount she knew of him, she had pictured him as slight and fair, with a thin sensitive face and a shy manner.

Nothing at all like Michele Diomede.

Now to find they were one and the same had thrown her completely. She scarcely knew what to think or feel. Liar! She felt angry, wounded, somehow *betrayed*.

Running through her mind, like a tape she was unable to switch off, was the newspaper story that Peter Sebastian was thought to have an American fiancée and would probably by staying in the States.

It seemed as if they'd been wrong about one thing and only too right about the other. She could even put a name to his American fiancée.

No wonder Michele's attraction to herself had been so *unwilling*. Unless he was a practised Don Juan, he must have felt torn and guilty. Or was she overestimating his feelings as far as *she* was concerned? Then again there was Didi's strange injunction to try 'being nice to the girl. . .'

Luce's bitter musings came to a halt as she realised they were approaching the back entrance of a sinister-looking building.

'The Ca' del Serpente,' Michele confirmed.

The huge black doors of the boat-house had been

79

80 JOY BRINGER

fastened back to allow free access. Greeny-brown water swirled round and through gaps in the wood, which was broken and jagged like rotten teeth.

Inside the boat-house quite a lot of the space was taken up by a flat, barge-type boat that had obviously brought builder's supplies.

On the stone loading-bay were bags of sand and cement, ladders, piles of scaffolding, and a bright yellow concrete-mixer, incongruous against the decaying splendour of its background.

Michele secured the motor-boat to one of the mooring rings and handed her out. For the first time she felt as though he was a stranger.

They crossed the jetty to a large wooden door, which had been propped open with a three-legged stool. Inside was a bare stone corridor, giving access to what would, in the old days, have been servants' quarters, kitchens and store-rooms.

No one was in sight, but somebody was whistling cheerfully, and above the noise of hammering a radio belted out pop music.

Despite the homely sounds, the place felt as cold and dank as a tomb. Her previous dislike in no way abated, Luce shivered.

Feeling the movement, Michele would have put his arm around her, but she drew away, deliberately distancing herself.

Ahead of them stairs led up to the main part of the *palazzo*, where most of the interior had been renovated and the air smelt strongly of paint and plaster and sawdust.

When they reached the massive entrance hall Michele waved a hand at the rooms leading off. 'I have first pick,' he said drily. 'So if you'd care to select the most suitable?'

Feeling oddly remote, detached, Luce walked through the various rooms as though on automatic

JOY BRINGER

pilot, weighing up the pros and cons: accessibility, what space was needed, how the lighting could be arranged, the desirability of an exit at either end. . .

Finally she made her choice and gave the reasons for it with the confidence she always brought to her work. The only thing lacking was her normal enthusiasm.

Accepting her decision without question, Michele nodded and left it at that, then, taking her elbow, he began to lead her back the way they'd come.

Stopping in her tracks, she stared at him with cool, blank eyes and freed her arm.

Usually so mentally attuned, so aware of what she was thinking and feeling, he looked angry and nonplussed, unable to understand her withdrawal.

She hardly understood it herself. After all, she *had known* of Didi Lombard's existence. Though had she, perhaps subconsciously, tried to ignore it—at least in relation to herself and Michele. . .?

They walked back without speaking.

When they reached the stairs, his voice determinedly reasonable, he asked, 'Do you want to return to Ca' del Leone to shower and change before we go out for a meal?'

'Thank you, but I don't want to go out for a meal tonight.'

Her cool dismissal stung, as it had been meant to.

Grasping her wrist, Michele stopped her in her tracks. 'What the *hell* is the matter with you? Why are you so upset? If I'd hit you you couldn't have looked more stricken. Damn it all, I'm still the same man.'

But he wasn't, and on some subconscious level she wanted to punish him for deceiving her.

'There's nothing the matter with me. Nothing at all.' She gave him that chill, remote look which she now knew infuriated him, and felt a fierce satisfaction to see him struggle for self-control.

Since they'd met he was the one who had been in

82 JOY BRINGER

charge, the one who had called the tune. Now the roles were reversed.

He gritted his teeth. 'I'd like to know exactly what goes on in that head of yours.'

She almost admitted, 'I thought you did.' Somehow she bit back the words and said, 'Will you please let go of me?'

As soon as his hold slackened a shade she pulled free and set off down the stairs. She had taken only a couple of steps when in her haste she missed her footing.

Unable to save herself, with a startled cry she pitched forward, tumbling down the remaining stairs and banging her head on the stone floor. The world exploded in a flash, brilliant as a magnesium flare, which was followed by blackness.

The blackness receded almost immediately and she became aware of pain. An excruciating pain in her head and stabbing agony in one ankle. In between it just hurt.

Michele was crouching by her side, his face taut. 'Lie still,' he ordered as she tried to sit up. 'Where's the pain?'

She told him.

'You silly little fool,' he said savagely. 'You could have been killed.' While he spoke his hands were moving over her limbs, checking for broken bones. 'Why in God's name did you go rushing off like that? If you'd taken more care. . .'

Luce made a sweeping gesture with one arm and tried not to wince at the pain. 'Put it down to my Sagittarian sense of drama.'

'I'm more inclined to put it down to your Sagittarian impetuosity and clumsiness.'

'How unkind.' They were sparring again, she realised. Though nothing had *altered*, somehow the fall had shattered the ice that had temporarily walled her

JOY BRINGER 83

up. 'And when I'm so fragile,' she added for good measure.

He snorted. 'You might *look* fragile, but. . .'

She lifted an ashen face. 'Yes, you're right. Really I'm as tough as old boot leather.'

'Hold still; let me look at that.' He examined the already darkening bump high on her temple.

She made a further effort to sit up, and groaned as a tide of pain engulfed her.

'Will you lie still?' he snarled. 'You might have some broken ribs.'

Gently he felt over her ribcage.

'It's a good job I'm not ticklish,' she managed. 'I think it might hurt to laugh.'

'If you weren't already so bruised and battered I'd turn you over my knee and make sure you had nothing to laugh about.'

His hands completed their task, and he added with obvious relief, 'Well, at least there doesn't seem to be any bones broken. Can you stand? And take your time.'

With the utmost care he helped her to her feet. She was only able to put weight on her left foot and, as soon as she straightened, her head swam and nausea engulfed her. Closing her eyes, she leaned against him weakly, her whole body on fire with pain.

After a moment she felt herself lifted and carried a few paces. Through the waves of dizziness that made consciousness ebb and flow she was vaguely aware of voices, of being transferred to someone else, then of careful hands lowering her into waiting arms.

She felt the boat rock, heard its engine roar into life, and then a cool breeze was blowing the nausea and giddiness away.

Luce opened her eyes to find that a burly stranger in workmen's overalls was at the wheel, and she was lying cradled against Michele's chest, her head on his shoulder.

Surreptitiously she studied that lean, attractive face, so close to hers, the austere yet passionate mouth above a cleft chin, the brilliant eyes so fascinating in their shape and colour, the clear-cut bone-structure, the strong planes and angles.

He was as beautiful as the dark angel.

A faint stubble roughened his chin and just beneath his jawline was a small crescent-shaped scar. He appeared deep in thought, his head slightly bent, thick, curly lashes almost brushing his hard cheekbones.

She longed to touch him, to trace his lips, the curve of his jaw, the smooth column of his throat. Perhaps she made a sound or some small movement, or maybe it was just the intensity of her gaze—whatever, she suddenly found those silvery-green eyes looking straight into hers.

Colour poured into her face in a hot tide.

He muttered something she didn't catch, then she felt the slight bump as the boat drew alongside the steps of Ca' del Leone.

'I'll get out myself. . .' she began.

'You will do *exactly* as you're told.' His tone brooked no argument.

Not that she felt up to arguing, she was forced to admit.

With the workman's help she was lifted from the boat and taken into the *palazzo*. Rosa came hurrying, and Michele gave the housekeeper some rapid orders before carrying Luce up to her room.

He must be superbly fit, she decided. She was no feather-weight, but even the stairs only made him breathe a shade faster.

When he'd put her down on the bed he said grimly, 'The doctor should be here shortly. In the meantime Rosa will come and help you get undressed.'

JOY BRINGER 85

'I don't. . .' she began.

He leaned over her, a palm each side of her. 'Any argument and I'll undress you myself. For the moment, at least, you're going to do as I say.'

'I hate to be bossed,' she muttered mutinously.

He grinned a little. 'Nonsense; it suits you.'

'It does not,' she denied crossly.

He lifted a hand and, touching her pale cheek with gentle fingers, gave her a heart-stopping smile. 'Oh, come on,' he said softly. 'You enjoy being mastered.'

She held her breath, waiting for his kiss. His lips were only inches from hers when Rosa's tap at the door made him lift his dark head.

As soon as Michele had gone the housekeeper began to help Luce off with her clothes. It was then that she missed her locket.

At her exclamation Rosa asked, 'What is it, *signorina*? Is something wrong?'

'I seem to have lost my locket.'

Rosa tutted in sympathy. 'Can you remember when you had it last?'

Luce tried to think back, but so much had happened. Finally she admitted, 'The last time I know for sure it was there was this morning when I was in Signor Diomede's office.'

'I'll make enquiries, *signorina*,' Rosa said soothingly.

Having gently and efficiently helped Luce into a loose cotton nightdress, the housekeeper was just tucking in the light counterpane when another knock heralded the doctor.

Dr Enrico, bustling and bearded, was equally efficient but nowhere near as gentle. His brisk examination completed, he strapped up Luce's injured right ankle and produced two capsules, a bottle of tablets, and a tube of ointment.

To Rosa, he said curtly, 'Give the patient the capsules immediately, then two tablets when necessary.

They will alleviate the pain and allow her to rest. The ointment should be spread thinly on the bruised areas. At the moment I can find no evidence of concussion, but any blow to the head can be potentially dangerous, so if there is nausea or blurred vision I must be called immediately.'

Picking up his black case, he addressed Luce. 'Stay in bed for two or three days, or until you feel well enough to get up. But don't put any weight on that ankle for at least a week.'

'*Grazie*. . .' Before she'd finished thanking him he was gone.

Having been provided with a drink, Luce swallowed the capsules before, clucking sympathetically, Rosa dealt with the bruises.

When the counterpane had been straightened and tucked in once more, the housekeeper put a carafe of water and the pain-killers close at hand and asked, 'Do you wish for anything else, *signorina*?'

'No, nothing else. *Tante grazie*.'

Rosa indicated a bell-push by the bed-head. 'Please ring if you need me.'

Master and housekeeper passed in the doorway.

Michele walked over to the bed and stood looking down at Luce. Gone was the lively, glowing girl of the morning, in her place a pasty ghost.

The oval face was white and pinched, a nasty swollen bruise marring the high, smooth forehead, the beautiful mouth was pale and the almond eyes looked dull and sunken. Even the dark hair seemed to have lost its shine.

Momentarily his jaw tightened, then, twirling an imaginary moustache, he declaimed, 'So, my proud beauty! I've got you where I want you.' Then in his normal voice, 'You see, I'm pandering to your love of drama.'

'Oh, is that what you're doing?'

'Now you're supposed to cry, "Spare me," or words to that effect,' he informed her kindly. 'Not that I will, of course. I shall ravish you to my heart's delight. And yours.'

Her eyes were on his mouth and, as though spellbound, she watched his lips forming the erotic words while heat suffused her body and her heart bounced about like a bumble-puppy.

Somehow she found her voice and said faintly, 'I don't think I'm strong enough to be ravished at the moment.'

'Pity. Still, I've given you something to look forward to. An incentive to get better quickly.' Then smoothly, 'How *are* you feeling now?'

'A great deal more comfortable, thank you.'

'Still in much pain?'

'No.'

He smiled thinly, recognising the lie for what it was, and, picking up the tube of ointment, studied it before asking pointedly, 'Is there anything else I can do for you?'

'No, thank you,' she answered. 'Rosa's done everything that was necessary.'

'Pity,' he said again.

Flustered, Luce added, 'She's been very kind.'

'What did you think of Dr Enrico?'

'He was extremely efficient.'

'But?'

So Michele was on her wavelength again. 'His bedside manner leaves something to be desired.'

'He's been crossed in love and isn't susceptible to women. That's why I asked for him rather than his partner who is, so I've been told, both charming and susceptible.'

Unsure whether or not he was joking, Luce said nothing. Whatever the doctor had given her was taking effect. The pain had faded into the background and she was starting to feel stupefied, her head stuffed with cotton wool, her eyes heavy.

'Sleep now,' Michele said softly, and bent to kiss her, the touch of his lips light as thistledown.

Luce slept for the rest of that evening and into the night, surfacing periodically as a racking stiffness made every movement torture.

Once she stirred, groaning, to find Michele standing by the bed, the single lamp lighting his body but leaving his face in deep shadow.

He put an arm behind her shoulders to lift her, and, when, not fully awake, she fumbled, held a glass of water to her lips while she swallowed two pain-killers. His black hair was rumpled, giving him a boyish look, and beneath the navy silk dressing-gown he was wearing his smooth, tanned chest was bare.

'All right?' he asked when he'd plumped the pillows and settled her down again.

'Fine, thank you,' she mumbled. She shouldn't enjoy this being treated like an invalid, she knew. But the mere fact that he'd left his own bed to come and check on her made her feel warm and cherished and oddly *weepy*.

He bent to brush her light fringe away from her forehead, his fingers gentle, before his palm cupped her cheek.

Perhaps he'd kiss her again. She wanted him to. Oh, *how* she wanted him to. But, his hand still lingering, he was straightening up. On an impulse she turned her head and put her lips to his palm.

She heard the swift indrawn breath of surprise, then he said softly, '*Buona notte*, Luce,' and was gone.

Her small gold watch showed almost noon when she awoke, refreshed and ravenous. She reached to touch the bell and within minutes Rosa was there.

'I'm sorry,' Luce apologised. 'You must have more than enough to do. Couldn't someone else. . .?'

The housekeeper shook her head. 'Signor Diomede said to take care of you personally.'

When the shutters had been opened wider to let in the bright midday light she helped Luce to the bathroom. Even with a well-padded shoulder to lean on, trying to hop was a jarring, painful business.

'I have it!' Rosa exclaimed suddenly. '*Signorina*, will you be all right if I leave you for a little while?'

'Of course.' Luce gave the assurance cheerfully.

Standing stork-like and hanging on to the various bathroom fittings, she cleaned her teeth and made a reasonable toilet. She looked longingly at the shower, but was forced to admit that for the moment she wasn't agile enough to use it.

She had just finished combing her hair when the housekeeper returned carrying a lightweight metal crutch, and began diffidently, '*Signorina*, I thought perhaps. . .'

'That's marvellous! Just what the doctor ordered!' Luce exclaimed. 'But where on earth did you get it?'

'It was mine, *signorina*. Last year I had a broken ankle.'

Using the crutch made Luce's return journey comparatively easy, and she was soon back in bed.

Having brought up a tray of pizza, salad and fresh fruit, from a capacious pocket Rosa produced the missing locket. 'I almost forgot. . .this was found. In the office, as you said. . . The catch appeared to be faulty, but it has been attended to.'

'Thank you, Rosa,' Luce said gratefully. 'I would have been very sorry to lose it.'

Young and healthy and spirited, now that the first shock had passed and the inhibiting stiffness was on the mend, after eating her lunch Luce would have got up if Michele, alerted by Rosa, hadn't appeared and put his foot down.

90   JOY BRINGER

'You're doing no such thing,' he informed her with dangerous calm.

There was a darkness in his eyes, anger simmering just beneath the surface. Anger that seemed out of all proportion. Unless it had some other cause entirely. . .

'You're staying where you are.'

'But there's nothing wrong with me,' Luce protested. 'I'll get bored just lying here. I'd sooner be working. Please?' she cajoled.

She thought his face softened slightly, but there was no relenting in his words. 'You're remaining in that bed for at least another twenty-four hours if I have to tie you to it.' Bending, he put his lips close to her ear and added in a threatening whisper, 'Or join you. I know I gave you an inducement to get better quickly, but I didn't expect you to be this impatient.'

Her cheeks hectically flushed, Luce avoided Rosa's eye and admitted defeat.

A television was installed in her room and a plentiful supply of books and magazines made available, but, annoyed by her enforced inactivity, she made a restless patient.

After dinner that evening Didi Lombard came in to ask how she was. The American was pleasant enough but it soon emerged from the conversation that the two women had little, if anything, in common.

They even viewed the world of art from opposite standpoints, and had totally different standards.

To Luce, a work of art was something intrinsically beautiful or fascinating, something produced with skill or merit that stirred the senses and provoked pleasure or sadness, or some more complicated response.

Didi judged whether a thing was good or bad by how much it would sell for. She respected money and hadn't time for anything, no matter how beautiful, that wasn't a success commercially.

'It's an approach that pays off,' she said decidedly.

'Since my husband died the gallery has become one of the foremost in New York. It's been hard work, of course. This is the first break I've taken in over three years.'

'How long will you be staying in Venice?' Luce asked as casually as possible.

'That depends on several things. But not too long, I hope.'

Probably just until the exhibition was under way and Michele could return with her, Luce reasoned with dull despair. Unable to think of anything else to say, she felt guiltily relieved when the blonde got up to go.

Some ten minutes later there was a tap at the door and Michele walked in. He came over to the bed and stood, tall and powerfully attractive, looking down at her. 'Temper improved any?'

Normally his provocative question would have sparked off a fiery response, but now, feeling gloomy and depressed, Luce said nothing.

He sat down on the edge of the bed and, taking her chin between finger and thumb, lifted her face to his and asked crisply, 'So what's wrong?'

'Nothing's wrong.' But her voice wobbled, and she felt dangerously close to tears.

'Just feeling low?' His tone had changed and now held an inflexion that could almost have been mistaken for tenderness.

Unbearably affected, she swallowed hard.

Seeing the betraying movement, his hand slid down to close lightly around her throat; then he touched his lips to the corner of her mouth with delicate precision before planting a series of soft baby kisses along the clean line of her jaw.

'Don't.' Shivering, she tried to pull away.

'Scared of what it might lead to?' he asked with gentle mockery.

JOY BRINGER

Unable to answer, she stared at him, her long-lashed golden eyes wide and vulnerable.

'You don't need to worry,' he told her with a rueful smile, 'we're quite adequately chaperoned. Rosa is a woman of strict moral principles. If she knows I'm in here she's probably hovering outside the door right now.'

'I hope so,' Luce muttered fervently.

He laughed and released her, sitting back. 'So what's wrong?'

She might have known he wouldn't let it go so easily.

'I've told you, nothing's wrong. I. . .I just don't want you to make love to me.'

'Liar. You *do* want me to make love to you.'

'I don't want to upset the status quo.'

'The status quo?' He raised a winged brow.

Lifting her chin, she looked him in the eye. 'It was reported in the Press that Peter Sebastian has an American fiancée.'

'So that's it,' he said softly. Then with unerring accuracy he hit the gold. 'But the night before last, when we were in the garden, you knew Didi was here and it didn't seem to bother you overmuch.'

Fighting back in earnest now, Luce said, 'I hadn't realised then that she was your fiancée. After what she'd said earlier. . .'

'Ah, yes. She said you were quite obviously smitten.'

Luce glared at him. 'She also said if you went about it the right way you could have me eating out of your hand.'

He looked at her quizzically. 'Then clearly I *haven't* gone about it the right way.'

Ignoring that, Luce demanded, 'What did she mean by saying such a thing?'

Michele's shoulders moved in a slight shrug. 'I suppose she meant if you were. . .malleable the. . .job would proceed faster and more efficiently. She's in a hurry to get back to New York.'

'Are you going with her?' She *had* to ask.

'That was my intention.'

Her heart felt as if it was broken. 'Well, you won't need me eating out of your hand to make me fast or efficient,' Luce said bleakly. 'I'll have the exhibition ready as soon as possible. I'd hate to hold up your departure.'

He sighed theatrically. 'If you would only *listen* instead of jumping to conclusions. I said it *was* my intention. *Was* being the past tense.'

'Well, if you *were* intending to go back to the States with your fiancée. . .'

'You're doing it again,' he complained.

'Doing what again?'

'Jumping to conclusions.'

'But you said——'

'I never said Didi was my fiancée. It was you who said that.'

'The Press said it.'

'Do you believe all you read in the Press?'

Luce put a hand to her throbbing head.

'Well, *do* you?'

'No,' she admitted in a whisper. 'But if she's not your fiancée, why were you going back with her?'

'I have business interests in New York,' he said briefly. Adding after a moment, 'Satisfied?'

Happiness fizzing and bubbling inside her, exhilarating as a fountain of pink champagne, Luce nodded.

Michele's fingers moved to hold the warmth of her nape and his mouth covered hers. Her stomach tightened when his free hand lightly touched her breast, discovering the shape, stroking the nipple through the fine material of her nightdress, making desire explode in her mind like a shower of stars.

If she was going to stop him, she thought, it must be

now, while she was still able. But she knew she didn't want to. . .

The knock brought Michele's head up. 'What did I tell you?' he muttered as the door opened to admit Rosa. Then with a sigh, 'Perhaps it's for the best. You're really in no fit state yet.'

How could he take it so *lightly*? Luce wondered. And was still wondering some half an hour later when Rosa had settled her down for the night but frustration, sharper than any pangs of hunger, was keeping her awake.

Having lain sleepless until the early hours, it was almost eleven-thirty the next day before Luce surfaced.

Thanks to the crutch, she was able to dispense with Rosa's aid. She was still a shade stiff but, due, no doubt, to the ointment, her bruises were considerably less painful and, her bandaged ankle stuck through the curtain, she even managed a shower of sorts.

Without too much difficulty she put on fresh undies and a cotton shirt-waister, then sat in an easy chair by the open window to eat her lunch.

When Rosa had taken the tray Luce picked up the crutch and practised hobbling round the bedroom. Catching sight of herself in one of the long gilt-framed mirrors, she decided all she needed was a parrot on her shoulder.

Striking an attitude, she scowled ferociously and declaimed, 'Aha, Jim lad!'

The sudden laughter startled her.

Michele was standing in the doorway, his dark face alight with amusement. 'How's it going?' he asked, moving into the room and closing the door behind him.

She sought to hide her nervousness with levity. 'Well, I won't be winning many races, but I'm reasonably confident of being able to keep up with any wounded snails I might encounter.'

JOY BRINGER 95

'Good enough. You won't need to be too mobile just yet.'

'No,' she agreed. 'Once I've managed the stairs I can sit down to work.'

Before she realised what he was intending he'd taken the crutch from her and propped it out of reach.

'Why have you done that?' she gasped, wobbling dangerously.

'For two reasons. The first, to give me a legitimate excuse for doing this.' As he spoke he moved closer and lifted her high in his arms, smiling down into her face as if he enjoyed the feel of her slender body lying against his. 'The second,' he deposited her gently on the bed and sat down beside her, 'to make sure you stay here.'

'I'm quite fit enough to work,' she protested. Then with greater determination, 'You can't *make* me stay here.'

'You weren't doing too well with the crutch,' he pointed out, 'so you won't get anywhere without it. And unless you promise to stay in bed I shall take it with me.'

'You're an overbearing, arrogant swine,' she cried heatedly.

He clicked his tongue at her in mock reproof. 'Now is that any way for a nicely brought-up young lady to talk to her host?' Derisively he added, 'And I'm sure you *were* nicely and conventionally brought up. In the main you have very good manners, despite your Sagittarian candour.'

'For candour read complete lack of tact, not to mention rudeness,' she said ruefully. 'I'm sorry.'

'For that gracious apology I'll allow you to get up for dinner tonight.'

'But it's *ages* until dinnertime,' she complained.

'Well, I'm sure we can think of something to do to pass the next hour or so,' he told her encouragingly. 'I

96   JOY BRINGER

don't have to go out until three, and if you're well enough to work you're well enough for anything.'

He lifted her hand to his lips and kissed the inside of her wrist, the tip of his tongue just brushing the skin.

Her breath coming fast, Luce said, 'I don't know what you mean by *anything*, but——'

'Don't be silly,' he chided. 'You know perfectly well what I mean.'

Ignoring the gleam in his eyes, she carried on '—but bear in mind that Rosa might walk in any minute.'

Michele sighed. 'True and inhibiting. We don't want to shock that good woman's tender susceptibilities, do we? Of course, I could lock the door, but that would almost certainly give rise to unwelcome conjectures. . .'

Turning Luce's hand, he bit the fleshy part of her thumb, making her whole body clench. 'So what do you suggest?'

She looked at the healthy gloss of black hair springing from a widow's peak, the thickly lashed eyes under winged brows, the mouth that could be austere and cruel but was now warm and sensuous, and said thickly, 'Perhaps we could go into the garden?' Anything to escape from this highly charged claustrophobic situation, to get away from this blasted bed and its connotations.

His lips took on a wry slant. 'The garden's a bit public for what you have in mind.'

'For what *I* have in mind. . .' Briefly she was left speechless by his audacity, then in a strangled voice she went on, 'All I have in mind is a breath of fresh air and to. . .to *talk*.'

'You know, Sagittarians are supposed to abhor false-hoods, but at times the lies fairly hop out of you.'

Luce choked on a retort. He was baiting her, of course, and she was rising nicely. She counted ten elephants, added two baby ones for luck, then said with

JOY BRINGER

sweet reasonableness, 'I thought you enjoyed talking. After all, you're a Gemini, a *communicator*.'

Smiling, he said softly, 'Between a man and a woman there are better ways of communicating than words.'

He watched her struggle to stay cool and unmoved, before adding thoughtfully, 'Though words have their uses. If I carry you down to the garden I shall expect your life story in full, a complete and truthful exposé.'

'Done,' she agreed unhesitatingly. Then, recalling that only a short while ago he'd guessed mockingly— and correctly—at a conventional upbringing, she added, 'Though you won't find it very exciting.'

'Let me be the judge of that.'

It crossed Luce's mind that, though he might be thwarted sexually, he sounded like a man who had got exactly what he wanted.

CHAPTER SIX

MICHELE stooped and lifted Luce. 'Put your arms around my neck,' he instructed.

Her heart beating erratically, she obeyed, clasping her hands together to prevent her fingers from straying into his black hair.

His profile was strong and patrician, his nose straight, the bronzed skin clear and healthy, the neat scroll-work of his ears set close to his well-shaped head. He was so good to look at. But his looks were only a part of it; it was the man himself who drew her like a magnet, his mind, his character, his spirit, whatever made him *him*.

One of the poets had said that first you fell in love with your eyes, then your mind, then your emotions. But she hadn't done it in stages. Instead of liking the look of the water, wading in carefully and finding it was wonderful, she'd tumbled in at the deep end. Now she was right out of her depth, not even sure she could swim, and both afraid and exhilarated.

Breathing in the faint spicy scent of his aftershave, she fought a wild longing to bury her face against his neck, to touch that smooth tanned skin with her lips and tongue.

He carried her effortlessly, and lying against his heart brought such vivid happiness that the journey down the stairs and across the courtyard was over much too soon.

When Michele had settled her on the swing-seat, her legs up, her back against one padded arm, he sat down on a bench opposite and, eyes narrowed against the sun, invited, 'Go ahead.'

'Where do you want me to start?' she asked. 'I mean, how far back?'

JOY BRINGER 99

'How far back can you remember?'

'I remember getting a clockwork donkey for my third birthday.'

'Fascinating. Do go on.'

'You're sure you won't get over-excited?'

'I think I can stand it.' His silvery-green eyes on her face, he prompted, 'The other night you said you were an only child. . .'

But all at once the light-hearted feel to the conversation had flown. There was an underlying tenseness in his manner, a *waiting*. . .

Normally Luce could talk about her life, her thoughts and feelings, her hopes and aspirations, with cheerful loquacity, even adding a touch of embroidery where necessary to provide a little more colour and excitement.

Now she felt strangely reluctant. A sudden intuition insisting that Michele wanted not innocent trivia, but for her to somehow *condemn* herself. To confirm his worst suspicions. But suspicions of *what*?

Watching a small, speckled lizard sunning himself on the trunk of one of the trees, Luce made an attempt to push her uneasy fancies aside and fulfil her half of the bargain.

'Yes. My parents had hoped to have a large family, but when I was born Mamma needed a Caesarean section. Something went badly wrong and she was unable to have any more children.'

Michele sat back and crossed his arms. 'Were you lonely without companionship of your own age?'

'Not that I can recall. Presumably what you never have you never miss. Or you compensate for it. Apparently as soon as I could read I always had my nose stuck in a book. Usually to do with art or travel.'

'Did you always prefer the arts to the sciences?'

'Always. Which was just as well. I didn't have enough brains for the sciences.'

'I don't think it was lack of brains,' Michele opined. 'Just the wrong temperament.'

'A pity you weren't there to tell my teachers that.'

Luce stretched and, having eased her ankle into a more comfortable position, went on, 'Looking back, I had a happy, sheltered childhood. Maybe a bit *too* sheltered. . . The only real sadness in my life has been that both my parents died young, and within a comparatively short time of each other.'

'Were you brought up to be religious?'

'Not in the conventional sense, but I was given moral codes of conduct to follow.'

'And you *do* follow them?' His tone suggested that he thought otherwise, and served to confirm her earlier instinctive feeling that he *expected* to find her flawed, contemptible.

Flushing a little, she said, 'I try to.'

Abruptly he leaned forward, his pose of idleness abandoned. 'How many boyfriends have you had?'

'Quite a few.' Attractive and popular, she'd had boyfriends since she'd been fifteen.

'What about lovers?'

Tension stretched between them like invisible wires.

'What about lovers?' She threw his words back at him with a different emphasis.

'How many of those have you had?'

'That depends on exactly what definition you put on the word lover.'

'The usual one. So how many?'

'Dozens,' she snapped.

'And did you get engaged to them all?' he asked smoothly.

Her lips tightened, but she said nothing. She wanted to get up and run; run as fast and as far as she could away from this man who seemed to be intent on humiliating her. But she was helpless, as well he knew.

JOY BRINGER 101

'Now there's a thought for the future,' he mused. 'Maybe all you need is a ring to get you into my bed.'

'It would take more than a ring to get me into *your* bed,' she retorted furiously. 'It would take chloroform at least.'

Not the slightest bit ruffled, he said, 'That remains to be seen. I think it should only take a few minutes to have you begging me to make love to you. . .'

A sixth sense warned her that he was deliberately trying to infuriate her, to make her angry enough to lose control. But why? Did he hope by that means to get at some truth he thought she was concealing?

'So how many times have you been engaged?' The soft, lethal question took her by surprise.

All the colour drained from her face and she faltered. 'Y-you asked me that the first time we met.'

'I'm asking you again. How many?'

A silken noose seemed to tighten around her neck. Should she tell him the truth, she wondered frantically, or stick with her lie? Swallowing hard, she said, 'Just once.'

'It seemed to take a lot of counting up.'

She stared at him stonily.

'Perhaps I should re-phrase the question.' His glance was cruel and barbed. 'How many *rings* have you. . .accepted?'

Knowing only too well that she had committed herself, that she was in too deep now to change her story, she declared, 'It doesn't make any difference whether you re-phrase the question or not, the answer's still the same.' Sudden, treacherous tears pricked behind her eyes. 'And it's the last you're going to get. I've had enough of this *interrogation*.' She swung her feet to the floor.

He reached her just as she made an attempt to stand, and caught hold of her upper arms.

102   JOY BRINGER

'Leave me alone.' She tried to knock his hands away. 'I'm not staying here.'

'You won't find it too easy to leave without my help,' he pointed out.

'I'd sooner crawl than let you help me,' she spat at him.

Infuriatingly he laughed. 'Talk about high drama. . .'

His move was swift and unexpected, and before she knew what was happening she was lying full-length on the cushioned seat, with Michele sitting beside her, imprisoning her there.

Upset and infuriated by such cavalier treatment, made miserable and guilty by her failure to tell him the truth, she gritted her teeth and stayed still and mute, trying not to blink as the angry tears welled up.

Sun slanted through the canopy of vines straight into her eyes, forcing her to close them and precipitating what she'd feared.

Michele's lips brushed first one cheek then the other, his tongue-tip gathering the twin tears.

Luce made a little choked sound, a protest that came too late. His mouth was already on hers.

Though far from casual, his kiss was brief. After a moment or two he lifted his head and, his face impassive, said, 'I must leave for my business appointment in ten minutes or so. Would you like me to take you back to your room first?'

Not trusting her voice, she shook her head, and, pulling herself up into a sitting position, watched him walk away.

Though the air was warm, she shivered, feeling chilled and desolate.

How could she have ever imagined they were two matching halves of a whole? She was a Sagittarian, open and naïve, a Pollyanna without guile or finesse who found it difficult to lie. He was a Gemini, complex

JOY BRINGER

and clever, a dual personality who could run rings round her with contemptuous ease.

Rings. . . That word seemed to be written on her brain in letters of fire. Why did he keep questioning her about boyfriends and engagements? He'd spoken as if he thought she was in the *habit* of collecting fiancés and engagement-rings.

Luce sighed deeply. At times, and briefly, they had seemed to be in sympathy, then without rhyme or reason his mood would change, the warmth, the closeness would vanish and he'd be deliberately cruel and wounding. . .

Her thoughts were interrupted by a step, and Rosa appeared, carrying a tray holding iced lemon tea, a bowl of fruit and a plate of almond biscuits. Several magazines were tucked under her arm.

She placed the tray on a round white metal table and pulled it closer, before handing the magazines to Luce. 'Signor Diomede said to bring you these, and ask if there was anything else you wanted before dinner.'

So he hadn't just walked away without another thought. A little warmth stole back.

'No, *grazie*. . . Oh, wait a minute, could you bring me the crutch I left in my room?'

'Certainly, *signorina*.'

Luce was sipping a glass of the refreshing straw-coloured tea when Rosa returned, accompanied by the cats, and placed the crutch within easy reach.

Secure in the knowledge that she was no longer quite so helpless, Luce relaxed and picked up one of the magazines, which fluttered open. A page of horoscopes caught her eye; she looked for the archer, and read:

With Pluto in Scorpio you have had an uneasy feeling that someone was plotting against you. Hidden hostilities have given you pause for thought. This period will start with still more doubts and uncertainties, and you have to make a choice that will prove decisive in shaping your destiny.

Of course, she didn't *believe* every Sagittarian had felt someone was plotting against them, or that each and every one had such a momentous decision to make. But, with regard to herself, the first part at least was uncannily accurate.

She gave a little shiver as a goose ran over her grave, and stroked Cas and Poll, who had joined her on the swing-seat.

Dinner that night was a strange meal. Luce, Didi, and Michele ate together, sitting around an oblong table in the dining-room of his comfortable apartment.

The atmosphere was anything but easy. Michele seemed aloof and oddly tense, saying little, leaving most of the talking to Didi and Luce.

Searching for something to keep the conversation going, Luce asked the older woman, 'Have you always lived in New York?'

'Yes. My grandparents were Italian emigrants who settled there in the early nineteen-twenties.' With a certain pride Didi added, 'My grandmother was a cousin of the Diomedes.'

Michele hadn't mentioned a family connection; all he'd said was business.

Curious to know how strong the ties were, Luce queried, 'Do you visit Italy often?'

'Not as often as I'd like. My husband was a native New Yorker, and I could never get him to leave the Big Apple even for a holiday. I must admit, I miss it myself, though I regard Italy as my second home. . .'

As soon as the meal was over Didi excused herself on the grounds of a headache, leaving behind her an uneasy silence.

Luce swallowed the last of her coffee and made to rise. 'I think I'll go to bed.'

'Not a headache, I trust?' Michele asked sardonically.

'No. I. . .I didn't sleep too well last night.'

'Neither did I. Frustration, I find, is a disturbing bedfellow. Don't you agree?'

Determinedly ignoring his question, Luce picked up the crutch. Before she could make any further move he was by her side.

'I don't need any help,' she said hastily. 'Really, I can manage quite well.'

'Walking on the flat's one thing; stairs are another.'

She'd been about to tackle that obstacle earlier in the evening on her way to get changed for dinner, when Michele had appeared and, despite her objections, carried her up. He'd returned some half an hour later to transport her down again.

Now, tolerating no opposition, he stooped and lifted her. 'You can bring the crutch, so long as you promise not to attempt the stairs.'

'It will be a great relief to me when I can walk normally again,' she muttered.

'And to me,' he said smoothly. 'All this propinquity plays hell with my libido.'

So his earlier tension had been sexual.

He moved lithely, carrying her with no more effort than if she'd been a baby. There was an air of intentness about him, a concentrated purpose that set a whole carillon of alarm bells ringing.

A sudden realisation burnt into her mind like a brand. When they reached the bedroom there would be no Rosa tonight to protect her, to save her from herself.

Frightened out of her wits, playing for time, Luce said in a voice that sounded thin and high, 'I've been thinking, I'd like to see your ancestors.'

'Tomorrow,' he promised, without pausing in his stride.

'Tonight,' she insisted.

Michele glanced down at her. 'Scared?'

JOY BRINGER

'Resolved.'

'Very well.' He turned on his heel.

Luce hadn't expected him to give in so easily, and she felt almost dizzy with what she assured herself was relief.

'I can walk down here,' she told him when they reached the long gallery.

He set her on her feet without a word and steadied her while she manoeuvred the crutch into position.

As they moved slowly between the rows of family portraits he explained who each member was.

'And this is the most famous of all,' he said as they reached the end.

Luce stopped and looked in fascination.

Side by side were two well-executed oil paintings of the same man. In the first he was seated, wearing ceremonial dress and the jewelled zoia of a doge. In the second he stood bareheaded, dressed in a swirling black cloak, fastened at the throat by a gold and enamel clasp.

The dark, clean-shaven face was strong and proud, the mouth firm yet sensitive. Beneath winged brows his deep-set eyes seemed to stare unnervingly into hers. Brilliant eyes of silvery-green with jet-black pupils. It was Michele, even to the slightly ironic expression and the long, well-shaped hands.

'The Lion of Venice,' Luce breathed. 'He's like you. Or, should I say, you're like him?'

Spellbound, she could have stood there gazing indefinitely if her ankle, which unconsciously she'd put weight on, hadn't protested with a stab of pain.

Seeing her wince, Michele lifted her, brushing her objections aside.

As he began to carry her away a half-formed thought, a prickle of awareness, came from her subconscious. There was something. . . She wriggled. 'Oh, please wait a minute, I'd like to have another look.'

JOY BRINGER 107

'Some other time,' he said, clearly believing that she
was only stalling.

Luce struggled to pin down the elusive thought, but
it hovered, wraith-like, just out of reach, and in a
minute or so was blotted out completely when she
found herself being carried into a strange, and clearly
masculine, bedroom.

'This isn't my room,' she said in a strangled voice.

'No, it's mine.'

'But I. . .I don't. . .'

He put her down on the bed, and, removing the
crutch from her nerveless hand, tossed it into the
corner, before sitting beside her.

Excitement spread tentacles that fastened round her
heart, squeezing it mercilessly so that it was unable to
beat, tentacles that compressed her lungs so they were
unable to breathe.

'What big eyes you've got,' he mocked gently with a
wolfish, better-to-eat-you-with grin, and bent to kiss
her.

She said thickly, 'I'm not ready for this.'

'You will be soon,' he promised in a husky whisper.
Then anything else she might have said was lost as his
mouth closed over hers, coaxing and exploring, while
with insidious magic his hands made their own light,
but devastating voyage of discovery through the
flowered silk of her blouse and skirt.

'"Licence my roving hands, and let them go, Before,
behind, between. . ."'

Luce had never felt so aware of her own body's
needs, never before dreamt of, let alone experienced,
such extremes of sensual pleasure.

She had said she wasn't ready for this. But she was.
Oh, she was! She'd been waiting all her life for this
man, this moment.

Delight, like some hidden spring deep inside, came

bubbling and leaping, so that her blood danced with it, and her mind became intoxicated.

Then suddenly, inexplicably, he was drawing away from her.

She made an inarticulate protest and tried to pull him closer, but deliberately he moved out of reach, leaving space between them. Cold, empty space.

Filled with apprehension, Luce opened heavy lids. 'What is it?' she whispered. 'What's the matter?'

His face set, his voice clipped, he said, 'I have to make sure this is really what you want. That I'm not taking undue advantage of your somewhat helpless state. I'll take you back to your own room now, if you say the word.'

Somehow she found her tongue and shakily voiced her only fear. 'If you don't want me. . .?'

'Of course I want you.' Momentarily his mask slipped. 'But *you* must choose whether or not to stay.'

'. . .you have to make a choice that will prove decisive in shaping your destiny. . .'

It wasn't a difficult choice. Without the slightest trace of uncertainty she said, 'I want to stay.'

She heard him release the breath he'd been holding in a sigh. Warmth came flooding back, and once again joy, intense and unbounded, went singing through her veins.

Still fully clothed, he stretched out beside her and drew her close, fitting her soft body to his hard one, making her ache for the complete union, where two separate entities merged into one and nothing and nobody else existed.

Pushing aside the imposed conventions, the restraints and inhibitions she'd always accepted as right and proper, *necessary* even, she pressed herself against him.

He kissed and caressed her, and with the delicate touch, the finesse of a very experienced lover began to

JOY BRINGER

109

undress her, slipping off her skirt before undoing the small covered buttons on her blouse.

Because it was easier than a bra and panties she had donned an ivory, gossamer-light teddy.

Quivering, she felt the moist warmth of his breath as, murmuring how beautiful she was, he nuzzled her breasts through the transparent lace.

Soon even that fragile barrier became too much, and he slipped the straps from her shoulders, gently easing the garment down.

She heard the sharp hiss of his breath, then once again he was drawing away from her.

Opening heavy lids, she found that he was staring at her with burning eyes, yet she was aware that he'd imposed on himself an icy control.

'Michele?' she whispered.

'It's too soon,' he muttered. 'I'm a swine to even think of making love to you while you're still so bruised.'

'But I. . .' She stopped and bit her lip, too innocent and inexperienced to know how to override his scruples, and too embarrassed to admit that, bruised or not, she *wanted* his lovemaking.

Her misery as extreme as her former delight, she lay perfectly still, trying to hold back the tears that threatened.

Propping himself on one elbow, he leaned over her. With the fingers of his free hand he gently stroked her cheek. 'I'm sorry, Luce. I shouldn't have rushed things.'

Settling back against the pillows, he drew her against him and, holding her as if she were egg-shell china, cradled her head on his chest.

His care and concern made the tears spill over.

'Don't cry, *cara*,' he begged.

'I can't help it,' she said in a muffled voice.

He sighed. 'I'm sorry if I hurt you.' Then in exasperation, 'Why the devil didn't you stop me sooner?'

110 JOY BRINGER

'You didn't hurt me, and I didn't want you to stop,' she muttered. Adding peevishly, and somewhat incoherently, 'I'm too old to be a virgin at my age.'

She felt his immobility, the stillness of utter surprise, before he asked carefully, 'Are you a virgin, Luce?'

'Don't you dare laugh!' she said fiercely.

'I wouldn't dream of laughing,' he assured her. Then, his mouth muffled against her sweet-smelling hair, he went on softly, 'Don't be too disappointed; I'll make it up to you. Tomorrow, if you feel well enough, I'll be more than happy to help you alter your status.'

The tenderness that emanated from him was balm to her wounded soul. Held against his heart, feeling the steady beat beneath her cheek, she closed her eyes and let it wash over her in soothing waves.

Luce surfaced in the early hours of the morning to find that she was still enfolded in Michele's arms. But now he was naked. The feel of his warm, firm flesh against hers made her pulse-rate quicken and every nerve in her body zing into life.

'Awake?' he asked softly.

'Yes,' she answered breathlessly.

'How do you feel?'

'Good as new.' She lifted herself on one elbow to peer at the clock behind him.

Lazily he enquired, 'What time is it?'

'Tomorrow,' she answered unhesitatingly.

He laughed softly, and his hand began to move slowly, seductively over her breast, the nipple firming immediately beneath his touch.

'No wonder you had me fooled,' he murmured. 'You're so *receptive*.'

But she never had been. In the past when any of her casual boyfriends had tried to deepen the relationship, having discovered early that laughter and gentle ridicule were the things most men's egos couldn't stand, she'd resorted to clowning.

She'd told herself that it had been self-respect, a dislike of casual sex, that had motivated her. But now she admitted that she'd simply been *unaffected* by them.

Though they'd each been special in their own way, neither Dave nor Paul had come anywhere near to moving her. There had been times when, feeling guilty about her lack of response, she had tried for Paul's sake to show some enthusiasm. But a show was all it had been.

In her heart of hearts she had wondered if she might be frigid. Now she knew without a shadow of doubt that she wasn't. The lock to open the door of her sensuality had only needed the right key.

'How did you manage to stay a virgin, Luce?' Michele asked softly.

About to make a flippant reply, she checked herself and instead gave him the exact truth. 'No one has ever managed to get through to me.'

Sounding taken aback, he said, 'You never cease to amaze me. But one of these days I'll fit the puzzle together and find out what kind of woman you really are.'

She'd thought almost exactly the same, reversing the relationship.

He kissed the corner of her mouth. 'Why did you tell me you'd had "dozens" of lovers?'

'Because I was mad. But I did say it depended on your definition of the word. The dictionary gives "lover" as an admirer, a suitor, or simply someone who loves, as well as its more accepted use.' Her voice had grown jerky and breathless and she caught at his caressing hand. 'You're distracting me.'

He smiled. 'I plan to do a lot more than that. I said I'd make it up to you, and when I make amends I do it *thoroughly*.'

She shivered at the promise explicit in his voice.

A promise that was abundantly kept. He made love

to her slowly and with exquisite care, wringing from her such an intensity of feeling that she thought paradise could hold no more.

Afterwards she lay in his arms in a haze of bliss until he sighed and said reluctantly, 'It's almost dawn. I ought to take you back to your own room.'

Getting out of bed, he shrugged into a bathrobe and handed her his silk dressing-gown. 'Put this on.'

She didn't want to leave him, but, unable to argue, to ask for more than he was prepared to give, she did as she was bidden, and gathered up her clothes and the crutch.

He carried her across the corridor and put her down on the bed. Slipping off his dressing-gown, she slid between the sheets and lifted her face for his kiss with the guileless trust of a child.

His mouth touched hers lightly at first, then he deepened the kiss with a passionate hunger that their lovemaking had failed to assuage.

She longed to cling to him, to put her arms around his neck and beg him not to go.

He knew. Freeing her lips, he smiled into her eyes. 'I'm not leaving you forever, only making sure the servants have no reason to talk.'

Running his fingers into her dark, silky hair, he cupped her face between his palms. 'I can't give you back what I helped you to lose, so I only hope you don't regret it, Luce.'

Her eyes glowed like liquid gold. 'I don't regret it.' Whatever happened, whatever the future held, she would never regret it. Many people lived a lifetime and grew old and grey without reaching the emotional and spiritual heights she'd touched.

He smiled, and asked softly, 'How did you get your name?'

'I was called Luce after my mother.'

'Light. . .' he said softly, 'it suits you. You're so full

JOY BRINGER 113

of light and fire that you're incandescent. Making love to you was like making love to a flame. I felt as if I were a phoenix, burning up in your fire, but eternally renewed.'

He kissed her again, lingeringly, as if he was as reluctant to leave her as she was to let him. 'Go to sleep now. I'll give instructions that you're not to be disturbed.'

'Michele. . .'

'What, *cara*?'

'Thank you.'

Just for a moment he looked as shaken as if her innocent words had been a knife thrust. Then he kissed her eyes closed, and promised, 'I'll come up for you about twelve-thirty, and we'll have lunch on the terrace.'

'Lovely,' she murmured, and was asleep before the door shut behind him.

Daylight was filtering through the shutters when Luce awoke to instant and complete remembrance. She and Michele were lovers! Such a sensation of pure joy filled her that she wanted to shout it aloud, spread the news, let the whole of creation share this sublime happiness.

She stretched luxuriously, and yelped. The spirit might be strong and rejoicing, but the flesh was weak and complaining.

A glance at her watch showed it was barely ten o'clock, yet she felt wide awake and as impatient to see her love as any Juliet. But, far from being able to greet him like a young girl when he came, she'd have a job to hide how decrepit she was.

The thought of a hot bath swam enticingly into her mind. Yes, that was just the thing to soothe her and relax sore muscles. It would mean taking the bandage off her ankle, but so what? She could always wrap it up again.

Some three quarters of an hour later she emerged

114 JOY BRINGER

from the bathroom, feeling refreshed and invigorated. Having rewound the crêpe bandage, after a fashion, she brushed her hair until it was dry and gleaming like dark spun silk, before donning a sunshine-yellow dress that perfectly matched her mood.

It was still only eleven-fifteen. How could she stay cooped up here until lunchtime?

Thankful that, though her ankle was still painful if she put any weight on it, her foot wasn't swollen, Luce put on a pair of yellow flat-heeled sandals and, unable to contain her impatience a moment longer, picked up the crutch and headed down the corridor.

Michele had asked for a promise that she wouldn't attempt the stairs, but she hadn't *given* one, and if she was very careful. . .

Even with one hand gripping the marble banister it proved to be far from easy, and when the stairs were safely negotiated Luce breathed a sigh of relief.

She went down the passage at a pace that would have left any wounded snails simply nowhere, and tapped at his sitting-room door. When that elicited no response she opened it and peeped in. The room was empty.

Perhaps he was in his office. If he was working she didn't want to disturb him. Maybe she could phone Aunt Maureen and tell her what had been happening. Well, *some* of it. . .

Purring loudly, Cas padded towards her, tail erect, bright green eyes unblinking. She stooped a shade awkwardly to rub behind a black velvet ear. His twin, perched on the back of an armchair, yawned, all white teeth and pink gums, then leapt down to have a share of the fuss.

A mock battle ensued—at least, she *hoped* it was mock—then the pair went racing soundlessly off to push the unlatched communicating door ajar and disappear into the next room.

At the same instant Luce heard the voices.

JOY. BRINGER

'. . . she's been here for the best part of a week and you're no further forward.' Didi sounded tense and exasperated. 'Surely you could talk to her? At least make her admit she's got it.'

'I've tried,' Michele answered shortly. 'But without success.'

'Well, you know he gave it to her. . .'

'Exactly. He *gave* it to her, which ties my hands to some extent.'

'He must have been out of his mind, giving a family heirloom to that cold, scheming little bitch,' Didi remarked bitterly.

'Not cold,' Michele corrected.

'She's certainly got the hots for you,' Didi said viciously. 'Though it doesn't seem to be getting you anywhere. . . So what's your next move?'

'I think it's time I put my cards on the table. Once I'm certain she's still got it. . .'

'You don't think she might have sold it?'

'No, I would have heard. When something of that kind comes on to the market it creates a storm. Most of the top dealers in the world would be after it.'

'So what will you do once you're sure she's still got it?'

'Try to get it back, of course.'

'But suppose she refuses to part with it?'

His voice as cold and hard as polished steel, Michele said, 'It was you who suggested I could have her eating out of my hand. . .'

CHAPTER SEVEN

STUNNED and appalled, Luce had stood perfectly still, transfixed, as though mortally wounded. Now she turned on her heel and, careless of the pain, headed blindly for the door.

Almost without knowing how she got there, she found herself in the garden. Instinctively avoiding the central area, with its swing-seat and disturbing memories, she followed a side-path.

Behind a screen of scented orange-blossom was a little arbour with a stone bench, and she took refuge there. Dry-eyed, shivering, in spite of the hazy sun, she huddled on the bench in a silent agony of grief too frozen for tears.

All the love, warmth and passion she would ever be capable of were his. And he hadn't even *wanted* her; it had just been part of a plan. A calculated cold-blooded seduction.

No, not that. She recalled the thud of his heart, the hiss of his breath, the hunger of his kisses. Though he might have *intended* to remain cool and detached, unmoved, it hadn't worked that way.

So he'd enjoyed it too. What difference did it make? His lovemaking had left her bemused and starry-eyed, a lovesick idiot ready to 'eat out of his hand'. Willing to give him anything. . .

His plan had worked perfectly.

A bubble of hysterical laughter rose to her lips. Except somehow he'd made a mistake, picked the wrong woman. It had been clear from the conversation that it wasn't something that concerned the *gallery*, but

116

her personally. And *she* hadn't got whatever it was he wanted, so it had all been in vain.

The only thing she could do was tell him so and leave for home as soon as possible. If he *did* want to mount an exhibition of his work—and she was starting to believe that that too had been a lie, just part of some overall strategy—then he'd have to find someone else to organise it.

Didi, for example.

Didi, who'd been so pleasant to her face and so vitriolic behind her back. But the American's comments, vicious though they were, had been easier to bear than Michele's.

They had left her bereft and emotionally destitute. But it was the knowledge that he'd deliberately set out to make a fool of her that wounded her the most. By holding back, pretending concern, he'd made her practically throw herself at him.

Perhaps when she made it clear he'd got the wrong woman he'd be sorry. . . But that was the last thing she wanted. His pity would be humiliating, *intolerable*.

So instead of admitting what she'd overheard, and letting him see just how much he'd hurt her, she'd play it down. Then as soon as he put his cards on the table she'd tell him he was mistaken, and leave. . .

'Luce. . .?'

Instantly she froze. She hadn't heard his footsteps. A shadow falling across the bench was her only warning.

'What on earth are you doing here? I've been looking all over for you. . .' Then suddenly Michele's hand was cupping her chin, lifting her face. '*Cara*, what is it? What's the matter? Have you hurt yourself?'

'No, I'm fine.' Her voice was as steady as a rock and she met his silvery-green eyes without flinching.

'You don't look fine. You look like a ghost. I told you not to come down those blasted stairs on your own.'

118   JOY BRINGER

'It has nothing to do with the stairs,' she denied with a crooked grin. 'It's more a case of the morning after the night before.'

His face softened. 'Yes, it was a bit. . .intense, given your fragile state. I should have——'

'Oh, I'm not blaming you,' she broke in. And, smiling, proceeded to tear to shreds the web of magic last night had spun. 'Even as a child, I was greedy and impatient. I remember being given a box of fancy chocolates, the kind of thing I'd never had before. Mamma warned me that they were very rich, but I took them up to my room and stuffed the lot. I was sick for three days.'

Gathering up her crutch, she rose to her feet and, apparently unaware of his stillness, added, 'I've never touched a chocolate since.'

Without looking back, she made her way out of the garden and across the courtyard. Though he moved silently, the slivers of ice sliding down her spine told her he was close behind.

Lunch was set on the terrace, as he'd promised, and Luce let him draw out a chair for her. He took his place opposite and leaned forward to fill her glass with Pouilly-Fumé. His dark face was expressionless, giving nothing away. But she could smell the danger; it drifted around her like a pungent perfume.

There was a tight, hard knot in her stomach that seemed to preclude eating, but in a gesture of defiance she helped herself to a platter of seafood.

'So you've gone off chocolates,' he remarked with a glint in his eye that made her even more wary. 'Does the same apply to everything you've been. . .shall we say, greedy for?'

The breath caught in her throat, but she was saved from having to reply by Rosa's approaching to say apologetically that there was a phone call, a business associate was on the line.

JOY BRINGER 119

'Excuse me.' Michele rose to his feet, and, tossing his snowy napkin on to the table, followed the house-keeper into the *palazzo*.

How long could she keep this up? Luce wondered bleakly. How long before she let the heartbreak show. . .?

Her thoughts were interrupted by the batting of an impatient paw. With relief she began to feed her seafood to Cas, who proceeded to purr like a small traction-engine. Poll appeared—the pair were never far apart—and ate his share in silence, except for the crunching of needle-sharp teeth.

By the time Michele returned and resumed his seat she was sipping her wine, her plate almost empty.

He eyed it thoughtfully. She was just mentally con-gratulating herself, when he remarked, 'You don't seem to have much of an appetite today. I watched you giving it all to the cats.'

The wine shivered in her glass. She might have known it wasn't that easy to fool him. . .'Ouch! Stop it, Cas.' Bending, she removed sharp claws from the area of dress that covered her thigh.

'That's what comes of feeding them at the table,' Michele remarked.

Luce took another sip of the crisp, dry wine and said nothing.

'You called him Cas,' Michele pursued. 'How do you know which is which? Didi can never tell the difference.'

Luce bit back an acid retort and explained, 'Though they look exactly alike, they act quite differently. For one thing, Cas always purrs, but Poll doesn't.'

'Ah!' Michele said, adding pointedly, 'And of course how something, or someone, acts can be a dead give-away.'

He fixed her with a look that demanded she raised her eyes to his. When, unwillingly, she did, he smiled

JOY BRINGER

and remarked, 'As soon as you're ready I have a surprise for you.'

His words alone were a surprise. She hadn't expected to be let off the hook so easily, but still. . .'I don't know if I. . .'

He raised a dark brow. 'I'm sure you don't want me to suspect you of cowardice?'

She shrugged. 'Very well, I'm ready now.' The sooner this masquerade was over, the better she'd like it.

'Come along, then.'

He escorted her across the courtyard, through the wrought-iron gate, and along the vaulted passage.

A gondola was waiting by the steps. As soon as Luce had been helped in and settled the gondolier plied his oar, and in less than a minute they were on the Grand Canal.

It was much cooler now, the sun had disappeared into a pearly haze and against the translucent sky the domes and spires looked almost ethereal, like a pastel-coloured frieze.

Everything was still, there wasn't a whisper of wind, flags and pennants and awnings hung motionless, and there was a strange *waiting* feeling, as if the very air held its breath.

Venice was unique, unforgettable, breathtaking in all its various moods, Luce thought as she looked over the calm water to the pale marble buildings lining the banks. Its beauty was timeless and wonderful, dwarfing her irrelevant appraisal of it, spinning threads of enchantment which drew people back time and time again.

But she knew with bleak certainty that, once she'd left it, she would never, ever come back. Sagittarians had a reputation for being insatiable travellers, and she was no exception, but please God she would journey to other places where there were no poignant memories.

JOY BRINGER

They left the Grand Canal behind them and glided through a labyrinth of quieter waterways. At the end of a narrow *rio*, the gondolier drew his craft into a small private landing-stage beneath a row of green trees, hanging like willows.

Michele helped Luce out on to a paved patio. He seemed to be watching her like a hawk, waiting for some reaction.

She looked around her curiously. The patio was flanked by ancient brick walls covered in climbing plants and variegated ivy. Behind her ran the *rio*, screened by trees, and before her stood—or, rather, *leaned*—a house.

It was a rambling old place, crooked and picturesque. Its long windows, their shutters fastened back, gave on to the patio. Steps led up from the stone paving to a wide veranda, which was adorned with hanging plants and tubs full of flowers.

Luxuriant creepers clambered up the walls to the pink pantiled roof, and even festooned the crooked chimneys and television aerial. An anachronism in such a setting.

'Well, Luce?' His voice cracked like a whip.

She glanced at him, startled. 'It's charming. It looks as if it belongs in some fairy-tale.'

'Is that all you have to say?'

'What do you want me to say?'

He gave her a dark, malevolent look, and, taking her arm, suggested, 'Come inside.'

The house appeared to be deserted, and suddenly she was not only reluctant, but downright scared. Clearly he'd brought her here for a purpose. . .

Luce shivered, her imagination suddenly starting to work overtime. She turned to take a reassuring glance at the gondola, but it was no longer there. It had vanished as silently as if it had been only a figment of her imagination.

JOY BRINGER

Aware of her unease, Michele smiled a little, a twisted smile that held no mirth, and, taking her elbow, led her towards the house.

She tried to rationalise things. So what if he did want something from her, something she knew quite well she hadn't got? Until he *told* her what it was she couldn't even deny having it.

But if she restrained her imagination and waited until he showed his hand, surely the misunderstanding could be cleared up and they could part as friends? she thought forlornly.

He helped her up the veranda steps and, taking a large key from his pocket, opened the arched door and stood aside for her to precede him.

The door opened straight into a cool wood-panelled living-room, which, though furnished with the most beautiful antiques, was comfortable and homely.

Filling the crooked fireplace was a huge bowl of fresh flowers. So someone must live here. Luce breathed a sigh of relief.

'The housekeeper's out, so we have the place to ourselves,' Michele answered her thought. Then, waving towards a low armchair, he added, 'Make yourself at home while I get some coffee,' and vanished through a door to the right that appeared to lead into an inner hall.

Instead of sitting down, Luce skirted an elegant bureau and hobbled across to a large bookcase. Books on medieval architecture and astrology were next to some good modern novels, a selection of classics, travel and adventure, mysteries, biographies and even poetry.

It seemed that whoever lived here had catholic tastes.

Her attention was transferred to the panelling. It was a work of art. At eye-level a series of beautifully carved rectangular panels depicted the sun, the moon and stars, and the twelve signs of the zodiac. Luce was

JOY BRINGER

studying them intently, when the click of the latch told her Michele was back.

She sat down, but not in the chair he'd indicated, and, pleased with this small rebellion, accepted a cup of coffee. He helped her to cream and sugar, then, taking his own black, sat down opposite and looked at her.

Trying not to let that bleak, destructive stare unnerve her, Luce sipped her coffee and waited.

'Well?' he demanded.

She lifted her chin. 'Well what?'

His dark, shapely head moved in a gesture that held tacit irritation. 'Does the place bring back memories? When you were here last time. . .'

'I've never been here before in my life,' she denied flatly.

Sounding weary, he said, 'Surely you must see it's no use prevaricating any further? I *know*, Luce. I know everything.'

'I only wish *I* did. But, as I don't, you'll have to tell me what it is I'm supposed to have done.'

Putting his coffee down with a violence that made some slop into the saucer, Michele jumped to his feet. He looked so furious that she flinched, momentarily convinced that he was going to strike her.

There was a fraught silence, then he sat down again and crossed his legs with great deliberation. 'Before too long you're going to admit the truth if I have to beat it out of you.'

She knew he meant it, and she shivered. Taking a deep, steadying breath, she said, 'I'd be glad if you'd put your cards on the table.'

His eyes narrowed to gleaming green slits. 'I did that by bringing you here.'

Her desperation only too obvious, she cried, 'But I don't know *why* you brought me here. I don't even know whose house it is.'

JOY BRINGER

'This is my house now.' His voice was tightly controlled. 'It was my father's. He lived here, remember? Shall I go on?'

'Oh, *please*,' she begged unsteadily.

Just for a moment he looked shaken, then he said, 'When you came before——'

'Wait. . .please wait, I. . .' The words tailed off. 'Won't you start at the beginning?'

He looked at her, his face like flint.

But if she was to *understand*, somehow she had to get a clear picture. She swallowed, and picked up his earlier statement. 'Why did your father live here rather than at the *palazzo*?'

He sighed. 'Very well, we'll do it the hard way. Though the *palazzo* is our family home, my father had never been very happy there. It must have been lonely for him. His marriage, which had been arranged by his family, wasn't a success, and, following a Diomede tradition, I was sent to England for my schooling.'

'You were an only child?' Almost before the question was out Luce regretted interrupting his flow.

But he answered, 'Yes.' And went on, 'When my mother died, ten years ago, my father did what he'd wanted to do for a long time and moved into here, leaving me the *palazzo*.'

'Does he still live here?'

The innocent query made a white line of fury appear round Michele's mouth. There was a pause, as if he was controlling his rage, before he answered, '*He died a few days after you left him*.'

'I don't know what you're talking about,' Luce whispered. 'You're not making any sense.'

'Last year you came to Venice for a holiday, and somehow you met my father. Overnight, it appears, he became infatuated with you. He brought you back here, and you stayed with him long enough to get him to part with the doge's ring. . .'

JOY BRINGER

One piece of the puzzle fell into place. So *that* was what they thought she had. And that was why he'd been so bitter on the subject of rings.

'I see by your face that you *do* know what I'm talking about,' Michele added harshly.

It seemed imperative to tell him the truth. 'Only to some extent. I overheard Didi and you talking this morning. . .'

'Ah. . .' he murmured.

She ploughed on desperately. '. . .And you're quite mistaken, believe me; I haven't got the ring. I've never been to Venice before, I can *prove* it, nor have I met your father. It *has* to be some other woman you want.'

He laughed harshly. 'I'm not a fool. Don't treat me as one.'

Naïvely perhaps, she'd presumed that he would believe her. For the first time she realised it wasn't going to be that easy. Suddenly she felt as if she was trapped in a terrifying maze, not knowing which way to turn.

Adrenalin pumped through her veins. 'I don't know what makes you so certain I'm the woman who——'

'Then I'll tell you,' he broke in. 'I was in the States when my father suffered a stroke, and by the time I got to his side he was paralysed and couldn't speak, which made communicating very difficult. But with the housekeeper's help—you remember Maria, the housekeeper?—I pieced together the facts that he'd met you, and within a week proposed and been accepted.

'He was convinced you'd only gone home to England to break the news to your family, then you were coming back to marry him. At least he was spared the knowledge that he'd given the doge's ring to a heartless little bitch who'd just taken him for a ride.'

Luce shook her head helplessly, terrified by the venom in his voice.

126 JOY BRINGER

'Or perhaps you "changed your mind", as you did over Paul and the others. . .'

'Others?' she whispered. 'What others?'

A white line of fury around his mouth, he lifted the gold locket around her neck and, opening it with his thumbnail, thrust it before her eyes. It held a head and shoulders snapshot of herself taken on her eighteenth birthday. Though the picture was small, it was clear and sharp. She had her left hand raised, brushing back a strand of hair, and on her third finger was a half-hoop of diamonds.

'There's one, at least!'

'How. . .how did you know?'

'Didi found your locket. She opened it.'

'She would,' Luce muttered. Then in anguish, 'I *wish* I'd told you.'

'If you're so innocent, tell me about him now, explain why you lied to me.'

Her heart like lead, she tried. 'Dave was handsome and romantic; I thought I was in love. . . It didn't take me long to realise I'd fallen in love with love rather than with Dave.'

'So why did you lie to me?'

'I-I thought you might not understand.'

'Oh, I understand all right.'

'I was young and silly, barely eighteen,' she added desperately.

'How old was. . . Dave?'

'Twenty-four.'

'You seem to go for older men,' he remarked cynically. 'But I find it impossible to believe you ever intended to marry my father.'

Her face like chalk, Luce said, 'I can understand why you're so bitter. But it wasn't me. . .'

As if she hadn't spoken, Michele went on, 'It took the firm of detectives I hired months to find you. You see, there wasn't much to go on, just your name, which

JOY BRINGER

127

the housekeeper remembered, a fair idea of what you looked like, and the fact that you were somehow connected with the art world.

'When Bonds told me they'd succeeded in finding you, and sent me a description that tallied exactly, my first impulse was to go to England and strangle you with my bare hands. Luckily for both of us, better sense prevailed.

'I decided it would be best to make you come to me, and devised a plan. If that hadn't worked I'd have tried something else, but, rather to my surprise, you snapped up the bait first time. . .'

Luce released the breath she'd been holding. 'So you *were* following me that first night, and you were in the Piazzale Roma to——'

'To take a look at you, and make sure you'd walked into my trap.' He laughed harshly. 'That should suit your taste for the melodramatic.'

She swallowed. 'Why were you following me?'

'Just keeping a general eye on you, trying to find out if you had any friends or contacts in Venice.'

'And it was you who searched my case and came into my room in the night and opened my bag. You were looking for the ring. . . But surely you couldn't have expected me to be carrying something so valuable around with me?'

Michele frowned. 'I didn't search your case, nor did I go into your room. As for carrying the ring around with you, that's not as silly as it sounds. It's so big that anyone who wasn't an expert could easily mistake it for costume jewellery.' With no change of tone he asked, 'Do you like the colour?'

'I've no idea what colour it is,' she said flatly.

She heard the breath whistle through his teeth. 'Damn you, *will* you admit the truth?'

'I've told you the truth.' She smiled bleakly. 'I just

128   JOY BRINGER

hope you haven't already paid your detectives, because you've got the wrong woman.'

He moved like a flash. Seizing her wrist, he hauled her to her feet and dragged her through the small hall and into a side-room with a wide, specially designed window on the north wall.

It was obviously an artist's studio, with stacks of pictures, some completed, some waiting to be framed. An unfinished water-colour was on the easel, but it was a canvas done in oils and propped against the wall that seized and riveted her attention.

Forgetting the pain clawing at her maltreated ankle, Luce stared unbelievingly at a head and shoulders portrait of herself.

The skin tone, the shine on the dark hair, the thick sweep of lashes, were lifelike. On the generous mouth was a half-smile which was echoed in the golden-brown eyes.

With savage triumph Michele said, '*Now* tell me I've got the wrong woman.'

The shock was so great that Luce was past telling him anything.

She took a step back and, gasping with pain, stumbled as her ankle gave way beneath her.

With a muttered, 'Oh, *hell*!' Michele caught her and, carrying her back into the living-room, put her down on the long couch. 'I'm sorry,' he apologised curtly. 'That was unnecessarily brutal. But this stubborn refusal to admit the truth would test the patience of a saint.'

After a moment he added caustically, 'However, I presume you're not going to try and deny that it *was* a portrait of you?'

She shook her head. Though it must have been copied from a photograph or something. . . But why? It was like a nightmare, she thought wildly.

JOY BRINGER

Making an effort to breathe deeply, to control the mounting panic, she asked, 'Who painted it?'

Michele's teeth snapped togther. 'You know quite well who painted it.'

'*You* did, of course!' she exclaimed. 'It's the only explanation that makes any sense. Though why and when. . .'

'My father painted it.' His voice was ragged. 'Now, while you're still relatively unscathed, I suggest we call a halt to this. . .charade. We won't talk about it again until you're ready to admit the truth.'

'I've told you the truth.'

His fingers closed around the soft flesh of her upper arms, as if he intended to shake her, then his face changed, the anger was leashed, and he said, 'You're shivering.'

'I'm cold,' she whispered.

'And in pain?' he suggested.

She nodded.

'Would you like to go upstairs and lie down?'

'No!' Then less violently, 'No, thank you.'

He got up and went out of the room, to return after a moment with a duvet, which he tucked around her. 'Even in summer the temperature can drop dramatically when these sea fogs roll in,' he remarked, before disappearing again.

A glance towards the windows confirmed his words and made her shiver even more. Opaque white mist pressed up against the glass, obscuring the outside world, and it was born on her how *silent* it seemed.

Normally there was a background hum of noise, but now it was as though the entire city had come to a standstill, halted and muffled beneath a thick, enveloping blanket of fog.

Somehow that made the situation seem a lot worse. Feeling cut off, isolated, beyond help, she closed her eyes in despair.

130 JOY BRINGER

'Here, take these.' Michele was back by her side. When he'd helped her to sit up he handed her two tablets and a cup of hot tea.

'Thank you.' She swallowed the tablets and sipped gratefully, a little warmth returning.

When the cup was empty he took it out of her hand, and said, 'If you're sure you don't fancy bed I'll light a fire.'

'A fire would be lovely.'

Her dark head on one of the velvet cushions, Luce watched him move the huge bowl of flowers to a side-table, before producing some kindling and logs from a metal-bound oak chest.

She was aware of the need to think things through, to find a way to convince Michele he was wrong. But she felt curiously light-headed, detached, as if she'd been pushed too far, and her brain had temporarily given up the struggle to cope with this Alice in Wonderland situation.

In hardly any time at all there was a satisfying crackling and an aromatic smell of burning wood as flames began to lick up the logs. A fire was comforting. . .

She awoke to find the room in darkness except for the glowing hearth. Michele was sitting in one of the armchairs, head back and tilted to one side. His thick lashes made dark fans on his high cheekbones, and firelight flickering on his face emphasised the planes and angles, turning it into a bronze mask.

He must have been as tired as she was, having undoubtedly had a lot less sleep. . .

Despite everything, she felt a sudden, fierce tenderness, as though with those brilliant, mocking eyes closed, and the hard mouth relaxed, he became a different man, a man who no longer thought ill of her, or wanted to hurt her.

'Feeling better?' he queried, opening his eyes.

JOY BRINGER

131

She jumped, and her voice squeaked a little as she said, 'Much better, thank you. . .' Unable to read her watch in the gloom, she asked, 'What time is it?'

He looked at the ormolu clock behind her. 'Nearly eight.'

Luce digested this in silence.

'Hungry?'

She started to shake her head.

'Rubbish,' he said firmly. 'You must be. You've had nothing to eat today. I'll go and see what I can find.'

Rising to his feet, he stretched, as sleek and graceful as one of his own cats, and switched on a couple of standard lamps.

It was warm and cosy; crimson velvet curtains were drawn over the windows and the panelled walls glowed darkly.

'I'd like to go to the bathroom,' she said. Then hurriedly, 'If you'll just tell me where it is I can manage with the crutch.'

Having shown her to a modern, well-appointed bathroom next to the kitchen, he left her. Luce washed herself and smoothed her fringe as best she could, scowling at her reflection in the mirror. Though the swelling had gone from her temple and the bruise was fading, she still appeared wan.

If only she had a comb and some make-up. It wasn't that she cared how she looked, she told herself. It was a question of morale. She hated to face him all pale and pinched, with heavy eyes and mauve shadows beneath them. But face him she must.

When she got back to the living-room the fire had been replenished, and a small table was set ready for them to eat.

Michele followed her in with steaming bowls of soup, a cheese board, and a selection of fresh fruit.

After the first spoonful of the thick and satisfying minestrone, Luce found she was ravenous. She ate with

132 JOY BRINGER

a will and, having scraped the bowl, murmured, 'Mmm. . .that was delicious.'

He grinned briefly. 'Although I say it myself, I'm pretty good with a tin-opener.'

When they'd finished their simple meal, obeying Michele's instructions, Luce moved back to the couch while he cleared away the dishes and brought in coffee, glasses, and a crystal decanter.

The atmosphere relaxed on the surface, taut as a bow-string beneath it, they sat sipping brandy, until Luce remarked, 'This house must be very old.'

'It once belonged to the Lion of Venice. Not to put too fine a point on it, this was his love-nest where he used to bring Lucia.'

'Oh?' Luce leaned forward, intrigued.

'He was a thirty-two-year-old widower when he met nineteen-year-old Lucia Lucchesi and fell deeply in love with her. She was on the point of marrying another man, so they could only meet in secret.

'It was, of course, an arranged marriage, and she knew her family would put great pressure on her to go through with it.

'But Lucia was clever as well as beautiful. She was an only child, and well aware that her father's dearest wish was to have grandsons. Knowing he was greatly influenced by astrology, she persuaded the most famous astrologer of her day to draw up horoscopes for herself and the man she was betrothed to. These horoscopes seemed to indicate that if the union went ahead it would be ill-fated and barren.'

'Did it work?' Luce breathed.

'Yes. With a great deal of diplomacy the contract was cancelled. Six months later Michele gave Lucia a ring, which has always been known as the doge's ring. . .'

Luce had stiffened at the mention of the ring, but Michele was going on '. . . and, a year to the day they met, the pair were married.'

'Did they have any children?'

'Two sets of twins, all boys, as indicated by the horoscopes drawn up for Lucia and Michele, which greatly influenced her father's decision to allow them to marry.' Quizzically he added, 'How much of the forecast was genuine and how much fixed, is a moot point.'

Smiling, Luce remarked, 'I noticed that the panelling is carved with the signs of the zodiac.'

'Yes, Michele had it done for his wife. Though they lived in what afterwards became known as the Ca' del Leone, it seems they spent some of their happiest times here. And later, when he become doge, he used this house to escape from the pomp and ceremony of the Palazzo Ducale, his official residence.

'They had a long and very happy life together, and when her husband finally died Lucia only lingered a few days before following him.'

Luce sighed.

'A love-story to please your romantic soul,' Michele said with a glint of mockery.

Silence fell, and for a while Luce thought about the Lion of Venice and his Lucia, and wished fervently that the ring would one day be recovered.

Then, becoming aware of how late it was getting, she asked, 'When will your housekeeper be back?'

'Maria's visiting her sister in Mestre. The weather being as it is, she'll no doubt remain there overnight.'

Luce froze, realising how easily she'd been lulled into a false sense of security. 'What will. . .I mean, will we have to. . .?'

'Stay here? I'm afraid so.' He smiled in a way that tightened every single nerve in her body, and added suggestively, 'But I'm sure we can think of *something* to do to pass the time.'

'No,' she whispered.

'I think *yes*.' Suddenly the gloves were off. 'You see,

my pride's at stake. I don't like to be equated with a box of chocolates.'

'But I wasn't. . .I mean. . .'

'Of course you were, *cara*.'

'Don't call me that,' she spat at him.

'You haven't objected before.'

Because then she'd thought, she'd hoped, that the endearment was. . .

Bending over her, he murmured softly, 'We'd be a great deal more comfortable in bed.'

'No! Don't touch me.'

'You look genuinely terrified at the thought,' he mocked.

'I *am*. Oh, please, Michele. . .'

'Do you want to talk instead?'

'If by *talk* you mean *confess* then the answer's no.'

He shrugged. 'I must admit, I prefer the first option.' Taking a box of chocolates from the bureau, he tore off the Cellophane, opened the lid, and with great care selected a fancy soft centre.

His white teeth bit through it. Smiling into her golden eyes, he ate one half, and put the other in her mouth.

CHAPER EIGHT

LUCE hadn't intended to take it; her lips had parted on a purely reflex action. Now she hesitated, toying with an almost overwhelming temptation to spit it back in his face.

He smiled grimly and said, 'I wouldn't advise it, *cara*.'

As the gooey mass melted she swallowed convulsively.

'There, that wasn't so bad, was it?'

'It won't make me as sick as what you have in mind,' she told him recklessly.

His jaw tightened. 'What I have in mind didn't seem to affect you that way last night,' he remarked. 'You actually thanked me.'

Her face flaming, Luce muttered, 'I must have been mad to let you seduce me.'

'You didn't *let* me. If you recall, it was your decision.'

'Is it my decision tonight?' she asked swiftly.

He regarded her with ironic eyes, his lips a little pursed. Lazily he answered, 'I think the lady should always be able to choose.'

'Then this lady says go to——'

He stopped the rush of words with a finger against her lips. 'Of course, I reserve the right to try and change her mind.'

Luce sat perfectly still, afraid of betraying her taut muscles by one careless movement. Her awareness of him was so intense that if his whole body had been dominating hers it would have been impossible for her to have felt more at the mercy of her own emotions.

His fingertip was gently following the curve of her

135

136 JOY BRINGER

brow, her cheek, her jaw, leaving behind it a trail of fire.

Without his so much as kissing her, a raging desire had seized her, and she longed to be in his arms, in his bed, in his heart.

All too easily she could be in his arms and his bed, but two out of three wasn't good enough. So it was a desire she had to deny. *If she could*. A quotation came into her mind:

'Desire, desire, I have too dearly bought,
With price of mangled mind, thy worthless wares. . .'

It was very apt. It expressed what she would almost certainly feel in the morning. But still she doubted her ability to hold out against him.

Every other man she'd ever known had left her totally unaffected. Such a complete reversal of her usual immunity only served to strip her of every vestige of confidence.

Yet this was a man who felt nothing but contempt for her, who thought her no better than a thief.

There was a curious burning in her mind; she wanted to obliterate, by some frenzied act of destruction, everything she felt for him. Deliberately she thought of the conversation she'd overheard that morning.

Taking a deep breath, she demanded, 'Do you deny you want to have me eating out of your hand?'

'No, I don't deny it,' he answered coolly. 'Though I'd have phrased it somewhat differently. I want you to love and desire me with the same degree of passion that Lucia loved and desired my namesake. And after last night, *cara*, I hope and believe you do.'

His words left her reeling, but somehow she fought back shakily. 'After last night I can't deny the desire, but as for *love*. . .' She invested the last word with as much scorn as she could put into it.

JOY BRINGER

Unperturbed, he said, 'When you're in the throes of passion I might be able to make you admit to it yet. We'll see, shall we?' He rose to his feet, wearing a faint aura of menace like a cloak.

Her heart started pounding and the breath caught in her throat. 'No, leave me alone! I don't want. . .'

Ignoring her protests, he stooped and lifted her.

Shivers crawled over her heated skin, her palms went clammy, and the blood drummed in her ears deafeningly.

Stairs of dark wood curved up from the hall, and the old treads creaked under their combined weight. The bedroom he carried her into had black polished floorboards, panelled walls and a high four-poster. But she took little heed of her surroundings; all her attention was focused on the man himself.

She had remained quiet in his grasp, offering no active resistance, aware that it would be useless.

Pushing the coverlet aside, he laid her on the bed, and sat down beside her, studying her white face. 'There's no need to look quite so scared.'

'I'm not scared,' she denied hoarsely.

'Rubbish. You make the pillowcase look as if it's been washed with Brand X. . . But I won't hurt you, I promise.'

No, he wouldn't hurt her, she thought bitterly. He would be heartbreakingly tender with her body while he crucified her mind and dragged her pride through the mud.

His kiss was neither violent nor demanding, more a gentle reconnaissance, and her lips remained immobile under his. After a moment he raised his dark head to look quizzically into the wide golden eyes fixed on him.

'No response, Luce?'

She stayed mute and defiant.

Smiling, he suggested, 'Let's see how long you can keep it up.'

138   JOY BRINGER

Bending his head, he kissed her again. This time it
was different. His mouth took control, its expertise
prising her unwilling lips apart, while his hand slid
inside the cross-over bodice of her dress, his fingers
relearning the shape and fullness of her breast, the
texture of her taut nipple, with a surety of touch that
made the blood race through her veins and bathed her
entire body in heat.

She tried to push him away, but she might just as
well have tried to move the Campanile. She *wanted* to
resist, she *would* resist, she told herself fiercely. But the
chemistry that governed sexual attraction had its source
in the mind as much as in the flesh, and all too soon her
mind betrayed her.

He picked it up at once. 'Do you want me to make
love to you, Luce?'

There was a tormented pause, before she breathed,
'Yes.' It was the merest thread of sound.

His voice a husky, erotic whisper, he murmured, 'I'm
glad it didn't take long to change your mind. No matter
what you are or what you've done, I can't wait to feel
myself moving inside you, burn up in your flame.'

But even so he stripped her without haste, all the
while keeping up a slow calculated assault on her
senses, until the only thought she could cling to was
that she mustn't reveal her love.

And to the best of her knowledge she didn't. Though
with hands, lips, and tongue, and an even more potent
weapon, he stormed her defences, ravishing her to his
heart's content, filling her with a delight so intense that
each climax was like a small death.

If he was insatiable he made her so too, and light was
filtering through the shutters before, utterly exhausted,
she fell asleep in his arms.

A finger tapping her cheek caused her to reluctantly
stir. With a groan she opened heavy lids, to find
Michele bending over her.

JOY BRINGER   139

'Coffee,' he said succinctly.

She pushed herself up on one elbow and, a strong arm behind her back, he helped her into a sitting position. It took a moment or two for her fuddled mind to realise that she was naked. Hastily she pulled up the sheet, and saw by the gleam in his eyes that he was cynically amused by her modesty.

He was already shaved and dressed. His black hair was brushed back from his high forehead and, still damp from the shower, curled a little around his ears and into the nape of his neck.

The coffee was hot and fragrant, and she drank greedily while he threw wide the shutters to reveal that all traces of the fog had gone and it was a clear, bright day.

Opening the door into an *en suite* bathroom, he offered, 'Would you like me to help you shower?'

Her lips tight, she shook her head.

He grinned mockingly. 'If you could see your expression! You look almost scandalised, *cara*, but there isn't an inch of that delectable body that I haven't touched and tasted, as well as seen.'

She blushed furiously, and inwardly cursed him to hell and back. Though it should be her own lack of will-power she was cursing, she admitted.

As soon as he'd gone she seized the crutch he'd brought up, and, hobbling into the bathroom, closed the door with a bang. If she'd said no and *meant* it she would have been safe. He wouldn't have forced her, she was sure.

Of course, he'd been clever, she thought wryly. He'd used a variant of the old "divide and conquer" technique. Instead of putting all her efforts into resisting him, she'd been more concerned about not admitting her love.

Yet though she knew she'd been a fool and totally lacking in self-control, still tangled in the sensual web he'd spun so effortlessly, she couldn't regret it. Leaving aside *his* feelings and motives, *her* feelings were so intense that if she could blot out the knowledge that he'd just used her, the two nights spent in his arms would glow like jewels in the ashes of the years.

When this bizarre situation had resolved itself, as it must, she would put her Venetian adventure behind her and take up the threads of her life once more. She was strong enough to carry on, to make the most of what she had left. Though she would always remember. . .

Never again would she be able to see a piece of Peter Sebastian's work, or think of Venice, without reliving this time. But surely one day the memories would cease to hurt? And perhaps that was all she could hope, that her pain, her regret for what might have been, would be anaesthetised.

She emerged from the shower, feeling greatly refreshed. This upstairs bathroom was better equipped, and, having discovered a toothbrush still in its carton, Luce borrowed some minty paste and cleaned her teeth vigorously. A spare comb pulled through her wispy fringe and below-shoulder-length hair completed her simple toilet.

Without bothering to replace the bandage on her ankle, she dressed, grimacing at having to put on yesterday's undies, and began to make her careful way downstairs.

As she got to the bottom Michele appeared in the hall, and said briefly, 'There's nothing to be achieved by staying here, so I've decided to get straight back. We've a water-taxi waiting.'

She had hoped to talk to him, to suggest that he ring Maureen, who knew quite well that her niece had never been to Venice before. But he was clearly in a hurry, so it would have to wait until they reached the *palazzo*.

Throughout the silent journey Luce racked her

JOY BRINGER 141

brains, trying, and failing, to come up with any logical explanation for the portrait. There must *be* one, but what it was was beyond her.

When they arrived at the Ca' del Leone Michele carried her straight to her room. He put her down in a chair by the windows and, his dark face abstracted, said, 'There's something I need to deal with. I'll have an early lunch sent up, then I suggest you get some more sleep.'

Before she could find her tongue the door had closed behind him.

She was tired of trying to think, and more sleep would certainly be welcome. They'd both had little enough the previous night. His enjoyment of her body had been intense and complete, his desire unabashed and unabated. If only that desire had been fuelled by love rather than lust.

She recalled his saying, 'I want you to love and desire me with the same degree of passion that Lucia loved and desired my namesake.' But for a vastly different reason. Not because that love and desire was mutual, but because he wanted the strongest possible hold over her. . .

Though she sat in a drift of sun-warmed air from the open window, she shivered.

A tap at the door heralded lunch. Luce ate the dainty chicken sandwiches and salad, then put on her fine cotton nightdress and climbed into bed with a sigh.

The last thought that flittered across her mind before she slept was that she would have given everything she possessed, sold her immortal soul, for Michele to have loved her as the Lion of Venice had loved his Lucia.

It was late afternoon before she stirred and stretched. She awoke with the Lion of Venice at the forefront of her mind, and for a while lay quietly mulling over what she knew about him.

Then, feeling a strong urge to look at his portrait

142 JOY BRINGER

again, she showered quickly, put on clean undies and an oatmeal skirt and blouse, and made her way to the long gallery.

Once again the tenuous thought that she'd previously failed to grasp hovered like a wraith on the verge of her consciousness. There was *something*. . .some shadowy impression that had touched her mind with insubstantial, yet unsettling fingers.

She looked at that lean, dark face, so like Michele's, and wondered what had disturbed her.

Her gaze dropped to his black, swirling cloak and she *knew*. Like someone in a trance, she gazed at the clasp that fastened it at the throat. It was made of two coats of arms on one vertically divided shield. The shield was of blue enamel. On the left were two gold lions rampant, on the right a dainty white unicorn with a golden arrow in place of a horn. The two halves, when clasped together, were united by a gold crown.

How long she stood there, transfixed, Luce never knew. She was brought back to reality by the pain in her ankle which, without her realising, she'd put her full weight on.

Turning, she hobbled back to her room as fast as she could and took her jewel box out of the drawer. There was no doubt at all that her mother's clip exactly matched the right-hand side of the clasp on the doge's cloak.

Was it just a coincidence? Strange coincidences did happen in real life as well as books, but. . .

There was a tap at the door and Michele walked in, tall and lithe and dangerous.

Hurriedly Luce dropped the clip back into the box and closed the lid. She didn't want him to see it until she'd had time to think.

'Have you been resting?' he asked, his voice holding only the cool politeness a host would show to his guest.

She nodded. 'Yes, I've slept for hours.'

JOY BRINGER 143

'Then you're ready to come downstairs?'

Luce hesitated. It was cowardly, she knew, but the thought of seeing Didi Lombard again wasn't one she relished. In her mind she could still hear the other woman saying lewdly, 'She's certainly got the hots for you.'

Knowing how the American had abused and derided her, could she hide her resentment and make polite conversation? Could she hell!

She started to shake her head. 'Really I'd rather stay in my room.'

'I take it Didi is the cause of your reluctance?' He clicked his tongue. 'And there I thought you had plenty of fighting spirit.'

'Oh, it's not *fighting* spirit I'm short of,' Luce told him drily. 'It's self-control.'

'I'd never have guessed,' he murmured with a sardonic smile that drove colour into her cheeks.

Trying to ignore the disturbing effect he had on her heart-rate, she said crisply, 'Well, if it's a fight you're hoping for. . .'

He shook his head. 'Though you're courageous enough, as far as aggression goes you're not in the same league as Didi.' Wryly he added, 'I couldn't allow my ewe lamb be torn to pieces by those talons. . .'

"My ewe lamb. . ." Of course, he didn't mean it, but just for a moment the implied tenderness in his words took her by the throat.

'. . .so I suggested that she cut her holiday short.'

Luce gaped at him. 'You mean she's leaving?'

'I mean she's left. I took her to the airport a couple of hours ago, after finding there was a free seat on a plane bound for London. She'll fly back to New York tomorrow.'

'But why? I mean, surely you didn't send her back because of me?'

'Indirectly.'

144 JOY BRINGER

Her brain whirling, Luce allowed him to carry her downstairs without further protest.

When she was settled in an armchair by the flower-filled fireplace, with Cas on her knee and a tray of tea by her elbow, Michele took a seat opposite.

He poured tea for them both and drank his before relieving her curiosity. 'I realised the situation would be a bit fraught, and there's no point in adding to the difficulties.'

His face darkening, he went on, 'Apart from that, she'd been interfering. You mentioned that your luggage had been searched and someone had come into your room during the night and looked in your bag?'

'Yes. . .'

'When I tackled Didi about it she admitted that she'd taken it upon herself to bribe one of the hotel chambermaids, a girl she knew, to do both. Of course, that was before she was aware I intended to bring you here.'

'Someone listened in when I phoned Aunt Maureen,' Luce remembered. 'I presume that was Didi?'

'Probably,' Michele admitted drily.

'But why did she?'

'Perhaps she thought she could learn something. She was as eager to have the ring returned as I was. You see, traditionally the eldest son of the family gives it to his bride-to-be, then eventually it's handed on to their eldest son. It seems that Didi was planning on it being hers.'

A twist to his lips, he added, 'I was thinking along the same lines myself when my father pre-empted me.'

Breathing with as much difficulty as if her lungs were full of broken glass, Luce asked very low, 'Then you love her?'

There was a long pause, before he answered obliquely, 'When I was young I fell in love. Francesca was as pretty as a picture and apparently glowing with health. I say *apparently*, because at nineteen she was

JOY BRINGER

diagnosed as having pernicious anaemia. I wanted to marry her regardless, but she refused. She wouldn't even agree to an engagement.

'She was twenty-two when she died, and I was twenty-four, and inconsolable.'

Rising to his feet, he walked to the window and stood looking out. 'But that's all in the past. I'm ten years older now, and in retrospect I see that if Francesca had lived we wouldn't have been right for each other.'

Turning to face Luce, his hands thrust into the pockets of his beige trousers, he went on, 'Last year I decided it was high time I had a wife and family. However, having learnt from the past, I determined to be detached, controlled, to choose with my head rather than my heart.

'Didi's beautiful and intelligent. We speak the same language, share similar interests. I respect her business flair, her acumen. We're. . .compatible in other areas. . .'

A tiny flame of hope that Luce had never even acknowledged flickered and died as his words, and the facts behind them, hammered themselves into her brain.

He might not *love* Didi, but he intended to marry her as soon as he had the ring, and he'd only persuaded her to return to New York to facilitate matters and save a possible clash. . .

Luce's thoughts veered. The American had presumably gone willingly enough, and it was she who had first suggested to Michele to try 'being nice to the girl', so she must be very sure of him. Though did she realise just *how* nice he'd been?

But Michele was going on, 'Only now I may have to think again, reconsider. After the last couple of nights, *compatible* hardly seems good enough.'

Luce sat perfectly still, her eyes on his face, her heart beating so loudly that she thought he must hear. She should have expected this turn-around. He was a Gemini, and it was all there when you knew what to look for: the cleverness, the ability to dissemble, the airy arrogance, the wry cynicism, the way he was expert at playing a double game. . .

He strolled towards her and, stooping, kissed her lightly on the lips, before saying casually, 'By the way, there's a letter for you. It was put with my mail.'

The blue envelope was addressed in her aunt's strong, distinctive scrawl. Luce tore it open and read:

> When I tried to ring you I was told that the Diomede number is ex-directory. After receiving your letter, Paul has also been trying to get in touch. Unable to reach you by phone, he's decided to come in person!
>
> Liz, who doesn't know him too well, said I should stop him! I did attempt to dissuade him, but without success. Having proved myself incapable of holding back an irresistible force, I now know exactly how Canute felt. I understand he'll be arriving early Sunday evening. Thought I'd better warn you so you can be prepared.
>
> Hope all is going well. Love, Aunt Maureen.

Luce read it through twice, and sighed. This was an added complication she could well do without.

'Something wrong?' Michele enquired smoothly.

She told him.

In no way put out, he said, 'In that case, you'll be able to return his ring and write *finito* to the episode.'

'I just wish it were that easy. You don't know Paul. I should have realised he wouldn't take no for an answer.'

'An admirable trait in some ways. I have been known to display it myself.' Michele gave her a mocking look, which intensified as colour came in to her cheeks. 'But in this case I think he'll see sense.'

JOY BRINGER

147

Moving to the fireplace, he touched the bell, and, when Rosa appeared, ordered briskly, 'Please bring Signorina Weston a coat, and pack an overnight bag for her as quickly as you can.'

As the housekeeper hurried away Luce asked dazedly, 'Would you mind telling me why I require a coat and a bag?'

'So you have the things you need for an overnight stay.' As her expression grew mutinous he added, 'We're taking a little trip, and it will probably get cool later, hence the coat.'

'A trip?' she echoed. 'May I ask where to?' She was up in arms, riled by his easy assurance, his certainty that he could manipulate her like some puppet.

'To Mestre. Maria's sister is ill, so she will be staying with her for a few days.'

It took a moment for the penny to drop. 'And you don't want to wait that long for an identity parade?'

'Exactly,' he answered drily. 'So, rather than drag her all the way back here for just five minutes or so, I thought we'd go there. Unless you want to make the excursion unnecessary by telling me the truth?'

Luce had been determined not to go anywhere. Now she said brightly, 'Certainly not. I can't wait to see Mestre.' And she couldn't wait to see his face when Maria denied ever having set eyes on her before.

As surely she *must*? Luce tried hard not to credit any other possibility, but the truth was, she felt like Alice, her confidence in the *sanity* of things shattered.

It was a beautiful evening, the low golden light slanting like beaten copper across the water and producing some lovely *contre-jour* pictures. But as Michele had prophesied, it was already getting cooler, and Luce was glad of her light coat.

They took a motor-boat taxi to the end of the Grand Canal and crossed the busy Piazzale Roma, with its juddering buses and crowds of pedestrians, to one of

148   JOY BRINGER

the multi-storey garages. Michele had phoned ahead, and his sleek silver Mercedes was waiting for him, the engine ticking over.

A young attendant in a blue uniform respectfully opened the door, and as soon as Luce had been settled into the grey suede luxury of the front passenger-seat they set off for the mainland.

On this occasion, the three-and-a-half-kilometre journey over the Ponte della Libertà was accomplished with ease and comfort. So much had happened that it seemed incredible that it was barely a week since she'd crossed the bridge in the opposite direction.

A week that had seen all her safe, conventional standards thrown out of the window, and irretrievably altered her life.

Mestre, Luce soon discovered, was a very ordinary town, with a thriving electronics industry, a modern shopping centre and lots of glass and concrete high-rise housing and office blocks.

'Not very exciting, is it?' Michele echoed her thoughts. 'But a lot of Venetians live here.'

Quietly she said, 'My mother was born here.'

From the quick glance he gave her she saw that had surprised him. 'Then your mother was Italian?'

'Half Italian, half English.'

'That explains how you come to speak Italian so fluently. I wondered about it, but somehow I never got around to asking.'

He turned into a dusty side-street and drew up in front of a five-storey block of flats. A group of youths on motor-scooters roared past, but otherwise few people were about.

Through open windows or balcony doors came the mingled sounds of pots clattering and televisions blaring, an indication that most families were having their evening meal.

When Michele had retrieved the crutch from the back

seat Luce followed him into the bare concrete building and waited while he knocked at the door of one of the ground-floor flats.

Clearly he was expected, because it was opened immediately by a thin, elderly woman dressed neatly in conservative black, her grizzled hair drawn into a tight bun at the nape of her neck. She looked harassed and ill at ease.

'Ah, Maria,' Michele spoke in Italian, 'I'm sorry to call at such an awkward time, but I won't keep you more than a minute.'

As she stepped back and opened the door wider he shook his head. 'Thank you, but we won't come in. You know Miss Weston, I believe?' he added silkily.

The dark eyes fixed on Luce showed dawning recognition, then puzzlement. '*Signore*, she *looks* like the other,' the housekeeper said after a second or two, 'but they are not the same.'

'How do you mean, not the same?' Michele queried sharply.

Maria answered steadily. 'This one is too young, *signore*. She is a girl, the other was a woman.'

'You're sure?' he demanded.

'Quite sure, *signore*.'

'Thank you, Maria.' His black brows drawn together in a frown, he turned away.

'Just a minute, please. . .' Feeling a combination of relief, incredulity, and intense curiosity, Luce found her voice, and, speaking in Italian also, addressed the housekeeper. 'The other one, her first name was Luce?'

'Signor Diomede called her that.'

'And she was very like me?'

'Very, *signorina*. But, as I said, older.'

'How much older? Ten years, twenty?'

'She looked comparatively young, but she might have been in her late thirties, *signorina*.' A thought seemed

150 JOY BRINGER

to strike Maria and she added, 'They always spoke English together, but once I overheard Signor Diomede remark in Italian how little she had changed.'

'Thank you, Maria. . . Oh, just one more thing, when was this?'

'Last September, *signorina*.'

Her thoughts tumbling over each other like clothes in a drier, Luce followed Michele back to the car.

His expression studiously blank, hiding his thoughts, concealing any reaction to what had taken place, he drove in silence, while Luce struggled to make sense of what she'd heard.

Only one explanation fitted all the facts, and it was so far-fetched that more than once she dismissed it. But it kept returning, boomerang-like, as the only possible solution.

When she surfaced it was to find that they were back at Piazzale Roma, the big square thronging as usual. Michele lifted out Luce's bag, passed her the crutch, and, having handed over the car keys, led her through the crush of people and vehicles to the steps that ran down to the Grand Canal.

The sun had set and dusk, like some nocturnal beast, had crept out of hiding and was stealthily licking its paws.

She had expected him to get a water-taxi, but he turned right and walked along the *fondamenta*, matching his stride to her slower pace.

A night breeze stirred the green creeper clinging to a wall, fluttered the awnings on an open-fronted stall selling touristy knick-knacks, and blew strands of silky dark hair across her face.

After a couple of hundred yards they came to a *ristorante*. A double row of lamplit tables bordered the canal, several of which were empty, but Michele led the way inside, remarking, 'It might be a shade cool out there.'

It was the first time he'd spoken, and his voice was

aloof, his dark face shuttered and remote, giving nothing away.

The *ristorante* was cheerfully garish, with red-checked tablecloths, plastic flowers, and raffia-encased Chianti bottles hanging from hooks in the ceiling, but the food was very good.

While they ate he made polite conversation, avoiding with care any of the deeper, more important issues that needed to be talked about and resolved.

Luce followed his lead, not yet clear enough in her own mind to try and provide any answers, or confide what she'd been thinking.

Suddenly, apropos of nothing, he asked, 'What made you decide your latest engagement was a mistake?'

Unable to admit that meeting *him* had been the catalyst, Luce said, 'I realised we were totally unsuited. Paul needs a clinging vine, a woman he can support and cherish, a placid, amenable, domesticated type with no outside interests, who'll be happy just running his home and watching television with him. When I thought about it clearly I couldn't see myself in that role.'

'Neither could I, ' Michele agreed. Then asked idly, 'What star sign does he come under?'

'Taurus.'

'That explains it. Taurus is the most uncomplicated sign of the zodiac; they're practical and phlegmatic, downright uncomfortable with the world of fantasy and imagination.

'Most of them seem to live quite happily in a rut, and put a settled home life and material possessions first. They often include *people* in the latter—at least, people they're fond of.'

Luce lifted a well-marked brow and prompted, 'Whereas Sagittarians. . .?'

'Are independent and vital, not particularly practical or domestic, and with wide-ranging interests. They hate to be tied down or confined, and they dream wildly

152   **JOY BRINGER**

beautiful, but sometimes impossible, dreams.' His voice had softened, grown almost tender.

'No, *cara*,' he went on after a moment, 'a Taurus man isn't the right mate for you.'

Nor was a Gemini. The thought was like a knife thrust. It was a perfect example of jumping out of the frying-pan into the fire.

'And I suppose you know which is?' she asked a shade wearily.

He smiled. 'Of course I do. Though I dare say, if I told you, you wouldn't believe it.'

She aimed for a light-hearted tone. 'Try me.'

Pursing his lips, he hesitated, then shook his head. 'Ask your Aunt Maureen.'

A thought struck Luce, and she stared at him, wondering.

'Well?' he queried with a lift of one black brow.

'When you decided to marry. . .did you take into account Didi's star sign?'

His eyes gleamed with sudden amusement. 'I did, as a matter of fact.'

When he said no more, curiosity got the better of her and she asked, 'So what is she?'

'You tell me.'

Luce thought over what she knew about the other woman. 'She's cool, clever, calculating, quite willing to talk, and well able to dissemble.'

'Very charitably put,' he congratulated her. 'So what's the answer?'

'Gemini?'

He took her hand and touched his lips to the inside of her wrist, sending a tingle like an electric shock up her arm. 'You're learning.'

CHAPTER NINE

WHEN the meal was finished the evening was still young, and they got a water-taxi without difficulty. Sunk fathoms deep in thought once more, Luce took no heed of her surroundings, and only when they were pulling in to a private landing-stage overhung by green willows did she surface and realise the significance of the overnight bag.

Michele met her startled glance and explained calmly, 'I wanted to make love to you, and I didn't fancy the idea of having to take you back to your own room in the middle of the night to save Rosa's tender susceptibilities.'

Rosa's susceptibilities couldn't have worried him overmuch where Didi was concerned, Luce thought waspishly. Or had he taken *her* back too? His housekeepers certainly seemed to rate more consideration than his bed-partners.

'What's that wry little smile for?' he asked.

'I just find it amusing that you're so considerate to your *housekeepers*,' she said pointedly. 'Going to Mestre to save Maria a journey, and taking such care not to offend Rosa's notions of propriety.'

His green eyes pools of limpid clarity and wholly deceptive depth, but his swift grin wicked, Michele replied provocatively, 'I can't make love to a housekeeper or beat her into submission the way I could a wife, and, as I prefer my domestic arrangements to run without a hitch, I have to tread circumspectly.'

Luce bit her tongue and said nothing. It would be playing into his hands to react to his deliberate teasing.

Entering the old house, she found, was akin to

153

coming home. Its atmosphere welcomed them, as though glad to have them back. Contentment scented the air like lavender, and the very walls seemed to hold memories and echoes of all the warmth and happiness it had sheltered in the past.

And this was Michele's inheritance, as Venice was his city. Belonging here defined him, made him free to wander, because here he had roots to return to, an anchor that gave him stability and a sense of permanence.

She envied him.

As soon as Luce was seated on the settee Michele crouched to light a fire, the fine material of his trousers pulled taut over lean buttocks and muscular thighs, riveting her gaze.

Finding warmth rising inside her that had absolutely nothing to do with the fire, she looked hastily away.

Once the logs were blazing merrily he straightened and suggested, 'Coffee?'

'I feel I ought to be making it.'

'Time enough when you're fully mobile.' His voice was casual.

He returned after a few minutes and put the tray on a low table by his chair.

During his absence Luce had had time to think about his reasons for bringing her here. She'd also had time to castigate herself for meekly following him inside.

His calm *presumption* that she would sleep with him infuriated her. Though she had her own traitorous desire to subdue before she could even begin to fight his.

Her guard up now, she prepared for the siege.

But when he handed her a cup of coffee and sat down opposite she saw that his face held the cool, ascetic look of a lawyer rather than the heated sensuality of a lover.

His voice quiet but as winding as a blow in the solar

JOY BRINGER

plexus, he invited, 'Tell me more about your mother, Luce.'

Oh, but he was clever! He'd either been following the earlier ramifications of her disquieting thoughts, or he was making a shot in the dark that, she feared, might be all too accurate.

Trying not to sound breathless, she asked, 'What do you want to know?'

'You mentioned she was half-Italian, half-English. Tell me about her parents.'

'Her mother was found abandoned as a baby, and brought up in an orphanage just outside Mestre; her father was a British serviceman.

'When the war ended he returned to live in Italy and marry his girlfriend, but after twelve years he deserted his wife and daughter and went back to England.'

'Go on,' Michele instructed.

'When Mamma was sixteen her mother died and she was left alone. Because she spoke the language she managed to get a job as nanny to the fifteen-month-old son of an English couple who were living in Venice. Gerald Wingfield was quite a well-known painter; his wife wrote novels.

'When they returned to England after two years Mamma went with them. In London she met John Weston, who owned the Ventura art gallery, which took most of Gerald Wingfield's work.

'He was thirty-eight, and a confirmed bachelor, or so everyone thought. But on their second meeting he proposed. In six weeks they were married, and ten months later I was born.'

'Did she come back to Italy often?' Michele asked.

Luce shook her head. 'She never came back at all while Dad was alive. I don't think he wanted her to. Perhaps he was afraid of losing her.' Now why had she added that, unless she'd subconsciously thought it?

'And when your father died?'

156 JOY BRINGER

'After Dad died she promised we would visit Italy together, but somehow we never did. We were up to our necks in running the gallery and it was always "next year".'

Michele's dark face was intent. 'But *she* came back?'

'Yes. Two friends of hers had planned to give their daughter a surprise trip to Venice as an eighteenth-birthday present. At the last minute Lesley refused to leave her new boyfriend, and they offered Mamma the ticket.

'She was desperately in need of a holiday, and Aunt Maureen and I persuaded her to go. I waved her off from Gatwick.'

His voice without inflection, Michele said, 'So last year in September Luce Weston senior came to Venice alone.'

It was a statement rather than a question but, her voice barely above a whisper, Luce answered, 'Yes.'

'And you two are. . .were. . .alike.'

'Very alike.'

His silvery-green eyes looked as cold as glacial ice. 'Then you knew all along that the woman in question was your mother?'

'No! No, of course I didn't. It wasn't until we'd talked to Maria. At first I couldn't believe it, it seemed ludicrous, but it's the only explanation that fits the facts.'

'You mean, she didn't tell you about——?'

'She didn't tell me anything,' Luce interrupted tightly. 'The next time I saw her she was dead. Killed in a pile-up on the M25 on her way home from the airport. I. . .'

Luce stopped speaking and sat quite still, her golden eyes wide, flooded with tears, tears that overflowed and rolled down her cheeks in two silent streams.

Sitting down beside her, Michele pulled her on to his knee, cradling her as one would a child.

JOY BRINGER 157

Just for a moment she sat stiffly, holding herself away. Then, giving in to the grief she'd always kept bottled up, she buried her face against his shoulder and wept like a baby for the mother she had loved and lost.

When at length she lifted her head and sniffed he produced a spotless hankie.

'I'm sorry,' she mumbled, having scrubbed at her face and blown her nose. 'It just seems such a senseless waste. Mamma was a lovely person and. . .' She stopped, then said fiercely, 'If you're thinking *she* would have treated your father like that you're quite wrong.'

'I'm not thinking anything,' he said soberly. 'There's obviously a great deal more to this than meets the eye. We might have been a lot wiser if, presumably to preserve their privacy, they hadn't always used English in front of Maria.

'But my father remarking that your mother *hadn't changed* implies they had known each other in the past, and the painting seems to confirm that. It isn't your portrait, so it must be hers, painted when she was a girl.'

'Yes, I'd come to the same conclusion.' Luce sighed, then said worriedly, 'The thing that concerns me most is what could have happened to the ring?'

'All your mother's belongings were returned to you?'

'Yes, everything. But it wasn't among them.'

'If she was wearing it there's always the chance that someone recognised its true value, and it was stolen.'

'Oh, no,' Luce whispered, unwilling to believe that anyone could stoop so low as to steal a ring from a dead woman's finger. But it was a possibility. After a moment she ventured, 'Do you think Maria would know if she was wearing it?'

'I can ask.'

Luce slid off his knee, and he picked up the phone and dialled.

It was answered quite quickly. Having identified

himself, Michele said, 'I'm sorry to trouble you so late, Maria, but have you any idea if Signora Weston wore the ring my father gave her? Do you happen to know whether she was wearing it when she left for the airport? You're certain of that? Thank you. *Buona notte*.'

He sat down again by Luce's side and ran restless fingers through his black hair. 'Though your mother wore the ring every day after my father gave it to her, Maria noticed that her hand was bare when she left.'

Luce released her breath in a sigh. 'But if she packed it it should have been with the rest of her things. You don't suppose the Customs. . .?'

Michele shook his head. 'When I realised the ring had probably gone back to England that was one of the first things I checked.'

His glance rested on her blotched face and swollen lids. Picking up her hand, he carried it to his lips. 'Don't worry about it any more tonight, *cara*.' Softly he added, 'Come and sleep in my arms.'

Lying close by his side in the carved and canopied bed, her head on his chest, she whispered, 'I'm so *sorry* about the ring. I know how disappointed you must feel. . .'

'There's no room for disappointment,' he denied firmly. 'I'm too full of relief that you aren't the mercenary bitch I took you for.'

Though his words could hardly be construed as an apology, and nothing had been *resolved*, Luce was so incandescent with happiness that she thought sleep would be impossible. But soon, lulled by the rhythmic rise and fall of his ribcage, his steady heartbeat beneath her cheek, she began to relax.

Cocooned in warmth, cradled in security, her last conscious thought was how good it felt, how *right*, to be lying quietly against his heart.

Luce awoke to discover a new day had dawned and

JOY BRINGER

was throwing streamers of sunlight, like bright yellow ribbons, across the dark polished floorboards.

She also found they had changed position during sleep and were now lying spoon-fashion, his arm draped over her, her back resting on his chest, her knees bent, her buttocks tucked snugly against him.

Her response was a sudden flush of heat and a clutch of desire that abruptly tightened her stomach muscles. The bedclothes had been pushed down, which enabled her to edge from under his arm without disturbing him. A foot of space between them, she turned on her opposite side to face him.

As she did so he moved over on to his back. He was still sleeping. Mocking eyes closed, firm mouth relaxed, black hair tumbling over his high forehead, he appeared younger, exposed, subject to the vulnerability that sleep brought.

She looked at him and loved him with a mixture of passion and almost maternal tenderness.

Though he might well marry another woman, he was *hers*, she thought intensely. This challenging, elusive, double-sided human jigsaw puzzle, with his empathy, his near-magical charm, his will-o'-the-wisp ability to play mental hide and seek, his loquacity, so oddly mixed with spiritual reticence, his dreams and his talent, was *hers*.

And he was *beautiful*. A rather feminine word to apply to such a very masculine man, but the only one that truly fitted. His dark, Renaissance face, his lithe, long-limbed body, even his strong, well-shaped hands, gave pleasure to the senses and the mind.

She let her eyes roam over him freely, and longed for her hands to have the same privilege. She wanted to stroke him, to run her fingers over that smooth bronze skin, to. . .

'Go on,' he invited softly, 'touch me. You know you want to.'

160   JOY BRINGER

Luce jumped and glanced up, but his lids were still closed.

When she made no move he asked teasingly, 'Have you any hang-ups about the woman occasionally taking the lead in lovemaking?'

'No, I don't think so.' Her voice was remarkably steady. 'Only, as I don't intend there to *be* any lovemaking. . .'

'*D'accordo*,' he said lazily. 'We'll do things your way. Just as far as you want to go, then, and no further.'

Perhaps it was the fact that he kept his eyes shut that made her bold. She edged a little closer and looked down at him, then, impelled by a need she could no longer deny, she touched his face, following the curve of his cheek, the enticing cleft in his chin, the finely chiselled mouth.

His lips parted a little, and she rubbed the pad of her index finger over the edge of his bottom teeth. Before she could withdraw it his teeth had closed lightly, trapping it there, while his tongue played over the sensitive tip. She gave a little gasp, and he released it.

Her pulses quickened as she ran her hand delicately along his collarbone, over his biceps and back to his chest. His skin was like oiled silk, healthily tanned and smooth except for a light sprinkling of curly black hair.

Having half expected that hair to feel crisp, to prickle beneath her palms as it had against her breasts, she was surprised to find that it felt as soft as down. Delighted, she stroked it, following the V to his taut stomach.

Then she caught her breath at the evidence of his arousal, but he stayed so still that, fascinated, she touched him, and felt the jerk of his response as she stroked and encircled his warm, hard flesh in an investigation that was both shy and bold.

She glanced sideways at him, and, realising belatedly that his eyes were open and he was watching her absorbed face, she flushed to the roots of her hair.

JOY BRINGER

161

When she hastily drew away and tried to wriggle off the bed he caught her wrist and pulled her back. Bending over her, he said softly, 'Not so fast, *cara*.'

'But you said. . .'

'I said, as far as you want to go. But you know as well as I do that you want to go a great deal further than that.'

'No, I. . .' She tried to find the words to tell him she *didn't* want to make love, to tell him she was totally opposed to such casual male dominance, but somehow they wouldn't come.

He rubbed his thumb lightly against her nipples, which were prominent through the material of her nightdress. His touch filled her with a thousand small, explosive sensations, and she felt as though every single bone had turned to jelly.

Bending his head, he began to kiss her slowly, leisurely, all the time in the world at his disposal. Her eyes drifted shut as he deepened the kiss, while easing the nightdress from her shoulders and freeing her breasts to his tantalising fingers.

Touching, nibbling, caressing every part of her body, making it his, he soon had her mindlessly receptive, totally forgetting any opposition.

When finally he fitted his lean hips into the cradle of hers she was ready for him, impatient for his possession.

Their loving was long and sweet and fulfilling, a meeting and mingling on all levels, making from two separate minds and bodies and souls, one whole and complete entity.

Lying contented in his arms, it was only as the euphoria gradually faded that Luce found herself wondering, had *he* felt the same? If he had, how could he ever contemplate marrying another woman?

She glanced at his face and found it engrossed. 'What are you thinking about?' she asked.

162   **JOY BRINGER**

His arms tightened. 'About you, my little joy bringer. . .'

Luce's heart sang as she recalled his zodiac sculptures, the way he had depicted Jupiter-ruled Sagittarius as a girl bringing warmth and happiness and pure joy.

'. . .and about the lovers this bed has known,' he went on. 'There must have been quite a few since Lucia and Michele.'

'Yes,' she agreed softly, and wondered if her mother and his father had been among them.

'Would you mind if they had?' he asked, just as if she'd spoken the thought aloud.

Luce shook her head. 'No, I wouldn't mind. You see, I'm convinced of one thing; if Mamma took his ring, she loved him.' In a muffled voice she added, 'They had so little time together that I hope they *were* happy.'

Michele rubbed his chin against the top of her head. 'Though we'll never know for certain, I. . .' Feeling her stiffen, he broke off. 'What is it? What's wrong?'

'Nothing's *wrong*. . . But I've just realised where we might find some of the answers we're looking for.' She was sitting up, pushing back her dark, tangled hair.

He sat up too. 'Where?'

She got a little of her own back. 'You're so good at reading my mind that I would have thought you'd know.'

'Unfortunately I can't always do it, only when it's fairly obvious. So are you going to tell me or do I have to force it out of you?'

Excitement colouring her voice, she said, 'Mamma kept a diary—apparently it was something she'd done since being a girl. I don't mean she wrote reams, but she always put down anything that was of importance to her.'

'Did she keep them all? Even the early ones?' he demanded.

'Yes, I believe so. There's quite a pile of them in her dressing-table drawer.' Luce swallowed. 'And one in the handbag the hospital returned to us. I. . . I did think I might read them some day, when I could bear to and it didn't feel quite so much like prying.'

Gently he said, 'It shouldn't be necessary to read them all. Only the early ones, before she left Italy, and the latest would be relevant.'

'Aunt Maureen has a key to the flat,' Luce said quickly. 'I'll ask her to send them. . . No, wait a minute, I've a better idea; she might be able to get Paul to bring them if she can catch him before he leaves for the airport.'

In a matter of minutes, wearing the light wrap that Rosa had packed, Luce was sitting on the settee next to Michele and dialling her aunt's number. To her relief the phone was lifted almost at once.

'Can you do something for me?' she asked without preamble, and went on to explain quickly what it was she wanted done.

'As I can't stop Paul coming, I might as well make use of him,' Maureen said cheerfully. 'Give me your number, and as soon as I know the score I'll ring you back. All this on the condition that you satisfy my curiosity later, of course.'

'It's a deal.' Luce glanced at Michele, who'd been listening.

Instead of dictating the number, he said, 'Let me,' and took the phone out of her hand. 'This is Michele Diomede, Miss Weston. You'll get us at either one of these.' He gave their present number, and the *palazzo's*, then added, 'Thank you for going to so much trouble. *Ciao.*'

'It's no trouble, Signor Diomede,' Maureen replied serenely. '*Ciao.*'

Knowing her aunt, Luce was aware that excitement and speculation were raging beneath that calm tone.

164   JOY BRINGER

Michele's grin told her he was aware of it too.

When he'd replaced the phone he said, 'I'll get breakfast as soon as we've showered.' His silvery-green eyes gleamed. 'Shall we take it together?'

Fighting down a swift urge to agree, Luce said firmly, 'Separately. I'm hungry.'

He laughed. 'Unromantic but reassuring. I'll get my own back for that later.' Tilting her face, he kissed her briefly but thoroughly. 'There's nothing I'd like better than to stay here and make love to you all day, but I think after breakfast we should get back to the *palazzo*.'

It was a fine Sunday morning. A warm, salty breeze blew in from the Adriatic and sunlight sparkled on the water as their motor-boat taxi carried them towards the Grand Canal.

All over the city church bells tolled and the locals hurried to Mass, while groups of tourists crocodiled after their guides, already appearing hot and tired and largely indifferent, snapping innumerable pictures simply because Venice was on the day's agenda.

It seemed incredible that it was only just a week since she'd arrived, Luce thought. Already she felt a sense of *belonging*, a need to protect this special place from the trampling hordes who came without any real *feeling*, who listened without *understanding*, and looked without *seeing*.

They had been back at Ca' del Leone a little over two hours when Maureen phoned.

'Everything's gone according to plan,' she reported. 'Paul's got the relevant diaries and his flight should be taking off mid-afternoon.'

Luce sighed. 'Thank you. Do you mind if I ask you something? You and Mamma were quite close. . . Did she ever talk about her life before she came to England? About knowing anyone special. . .a man?'

'Only once. I understand she told John the same

story before she promised to marry him, then they agreed it should never be mentioned again.

'When she was just seventeen she fell in love with someone quite a bit older than she was. He loved her too, but there was no future in it. You see, he was already married, with a child. I believe that was the reason she came to England with the Wingfields.'

Excitement making her voice hoarse, Luce asked, 'You don't happen to know what the man's name was, do you?'

'No, she never told me that. Why do you want to know after all this time?'

'Because when Mamma was in Venice last year I think she met the same man. They were both free then, and must have still felt something for each other. Apparently she agreed to marry him and he gave her a very valuable ring. A ring that seems to have disappeared. It wasn't with her things. . .'

'How come you're so sure that's what happened if you don't know who the man is?'

'We. . .I do know who the man is.'

'It can't be Signor Diomede—he's far too young.'

'No, it was his father.'

'I *see*,' Maureen said slowly. 'Fate works in mysterious ways. But if the man in question was Signor Diomede's father, why can't you ask him what you want to know?'

'He died of a stroke only a short time after Mamma left him.'

'They passed away within days of each other? How very strange. . . So you want to see if the diaries confirm any of this?'

'Yes. . .and maybe even throw some light on what happened to the ring. Though that might be too much to hope for.'

'You'll let me know what happens?'

'Of course.'

166 JOY BRINGER

It was almost seven o'clock when Paul arrived at the *palazzo*. Rosa showed him into the living-room, where Luce was waiting with mixed feelings.

'Paul. . .' She rose to her feet. In so short a time she'd forgotten just how big he was.

'Darling!' Taken by surprise, she offered no resistance when he strode over and, clasping her in his arms, kissed her firmly on the lips. 'I've been trying to get hold of you to see what all this nonsense is about. I'm quite sure you don't mean it, but I——'

Freeing herself, Luce responded quietly, 'I'm very sorry, Paul, but it isn't nonsense, and I *do* mean it.'

He shook his head. 'Once you get back home you'll see things in a different light.'

Fighting down the customary surge of frustration, Luce turned to Michele, who, having thrown aside the paper he'd been reading, was standing quietly, his expression politely detached. She took a deep breath, and said, 'May I introduce Paul Jenkins. . .? Paul, this is Michele Diomede.'

Both men were casually dressed, Michele in light fawn trousers and a black polo-necked shirt, Paul in brown cords and a beige anorak-type cotton jacket.

The two shook hands and silently measured each other up, Paul overtly, as was his style, Michele with more subtlety, a cool detachment in his silvery-green eyes.

As they stood together there could hardly have been a greater contrast. Both were tall and broad-shouldered, but there any resemblance ended. Michele was lean and darkly handsome, with a proud, patrician face and an unmistakable air of authority. Paul was a couple of stones heavier, blond and blue-eyed, good-looking in a ruddy, boyish way.

Michele was smiling slightly, but Paul wore a scowl, and it was apparent to Luce that, faced with the other

JOY BRINGER

man's cool sophistication, he felt ill at ease, out of his depth.

'Welcome to Ca' del Leone,' Michele said civilly. 'I hope you'll join us for dinner?'

'Thanks,' Paul replied stiffly, 'but I was planning to take Luce to my hotel for a meal. We have a lot to talk about.'

'I doubt it,' Michele disagreed. 'My understanding is that Luce said everything that needed saying in the letter she wrote to you.'

Paul began to bluster. 'My fiancée——'

'Your *ex*-fiancée,' Michele corrected.

Though normally good-natured and easygoing, Paul hated to be at a disadvantage. Now he was, and it made him belligerent. 'Why don't you keep your nose out of this?' he demanded furiously. 'Luce agreed to marry me and——'

'And she changed her mind.'

Paul tried again. 'She left wearing my ring——'

'But she isn't wearing it now,' Michele pointed out. 'Luce is fond of you and she doesn't want to hurt you, but you're putting her in an impossible situation by your pig-headedness. It's really time you learnt to take no for an answer.'

His face beetroot-red, Paul exploded. 'What the hell has it got to do with you?'

'Quite a lot.' Michele was unruffled. 'I am Luce's lover. Which is something *you* never were.' Then, hammering home his point, 'And she had no need to *tell* me that.'

'Why, you. . .' Paul took a threatening step forward, then paused, his big hands clenched into fists of rage.

Michele stood his ground without moving a muscle, and advised quietly, 'I think you should leave now. If you don't——'

'I suppose you'll ring for your servants and have me thrown out?' Paul sneered.

168 JOY BRINGER

'That won't be necessary.' Michele eyed his adversary calmly. 'I can throw you out myself should the need arise. Though, for Luce's sake, I hope it won't.'

Both of them turned to look at her. Flushed and harassed, she felt rather like a bone two dogs were snarling over.

His blue eyes suddenly anguished, Paul asked, '*Is* he your lover?'

Lifting her chin, she answered steadily, 'Yes, he is.'

'I bet the cold, unfeeling swine took advantage of you, seduced you——'

'No,' she said clearly. 'It was my choice.'

'You must have taken leave of your senses,' Paul cried. 'I suppose he promised to marry you?'

She shook her head.

'That's just as well, because he won't, that kind never do. . .' Suddenly his anger turned to pleading. 'There's no future in it, Luce; change your mind again and come home with me now.'

'I'm sorry, Paul, I can't.' Miserably she added, 'I shouldn't have accepted your ring. Please believe I never meant to hurt you.'

'I know you didn't *mean* to. . . Oh, well, I suppose there's no point hanging around here.' A dejected slump to his heavy shoulders, he headed for the door.

'Just a minute,' Michele's voice stopped him. 'Don't go without this.' He tossed a glittering object through the air.

Paul caught the ring, gave it a cursory glance and thrust it into his pocket, at the same time pulling out a small parcel. 'I forgot, Maureen asked me to bring this.'

He thrust the flat package into Luce's hand and the next second the door banged behind him.

Feeling Paul's desolation keenly, she sank on to the settee, gazing at the closed door.

Michele dropped down beside her. 'Well, that's that.

JOY BRINGER

169

I think he finally got the message.' His satisfaction jarred.

'Did you have to be so cruel?' she flared at him.

'Did you want him to keep on hoping?'

'No, of course I didn't. . . But I still think it was wrong to. . .to take away his pride like that.'

'All I did was tell him the truth.'

'It was the unkind way you told him.'

'Is there a kind way to tell a man the woman he considered his is really yours?'

It was no use, Luce thought distractedly. At the moment they were completely out of tune.

When she failed to answer Michele suggested, 'Let's forget it for now and eat.'

She shook her head. 'I'm not hungry. I'd prefer to go to my room.'

Momentarily he looked annoyed, and Luce sighed, knowing he had every right to. Seeing she was getting nowhere with Paul, he had taken over and saved her from having to cope with a great deal of harassment. She should be grateful, but somehow she found herself blaming him.

'Very well,' he said, his green eyes cool. 'I'll take you up.'

'There's no need. I can walk almost normally by now.' And it was the truth. Her ankle was still a shade painful, but it was bearing her weight.

Without another word she turned and made her way upstairs, using the crutch only as an added safety precaution.

Once in her room she took a seat by the windows and, pushing her distress over Paul to the back of her mind, tore open the packet he'd given her.

CHAPTER TEN

INSIDE were four small diaries, three of them the cheap cardboard-backed variety, the fourth a blue leather-bound volume that Luce recognised.

The first one had been started when her mother was just turned sixteen. The entries, written in Italian with a cheap ballpoint pen, gave a clear picture of a young girl who was desperately lonely after the death of her mother, but who refused to give way and feel sorry for herself.

It went on to tell of her relief at getting a job as nanny to the Wingfields, and gave an account of their daily life.

Just as Luce reached the end there was a knock, and Rosa came in, carrying a dinner-tray.

'I'm sorry to give you all this trouble,' Luce told her, flustered. 'I really didn't want anything to eat.'

'Signor Diomede ordered me to bring it up, *Signorina*.' As far as Rosa was concerned, that settled the matter. 'He said to tell you not to forget that you're supposed to be. . .' she hesitated, plainly uncertain, before adding '. . .the vulture variety.'

Cursing Michele's sense of humour, Luce hastened to assure her, 'It's all right, it's a joke.'

'Oh.' Rosa looked relieved.

When the housekeeper had gone Luce was about to push the tray aside when the appetising smell of beef and peppers and tomatoes stayed her hand. She hadn't thought she could stomach anything, but now that it was placed in front of her. . .

As soon as she'd finished eating Luce moved the tray on to a side-table and, not without a pang, began to

JOY BRINGER

read the second diary, followed by the third. They poignantly confirmed what Maureen had already told her. The young Luce had written:

Though he's a wealthy man from a good family and I'm a nobody, Lorenzo and I love each other deeply. We are truly soul mates. But it's too late. He's already married, and can never leave his wife and son, so for all our sakes I must go away. If I stayed, the temptation to be together might prove too strong.

Then about a month later:

The Wingfields are returning to England and have asked me to go with them. This has to be the solution I was looking for.

There was a series of blank pages, as if it had been too painful to write, before she went on:

We leave for England tomorrow. Lorenzo and I have said our goodbyes. I've promised him that I will make a new life for myself and not think of the past.
He gave me one half of a clasp that belonged to the Lion of Venice. The other half he kept. He told me that his happiness was leaving with me and. . . It's no use, I can't write any more. . . I love him. I love him so. Oh, dear God, how am I going to live without him. . .? But somehow I must.

Luce put the diary down and brushed away her tears. So it hadn't been a coincidence. The clip she had in her jewel case *was* the same one that appeared in the doge's portrait. She had wondered about it briefly when it seemed certain that her mother and Michele's father had known each other in the past.
She must show Michele when he came. But even as the thought went through her mind Luce knew with the

utmost certainty that *he* wouldn't come to *her*. *She* would have to go to *him*.

Stumbling to her feet, she picked up the diaries, slipped the clip into the pocket of her dress, and hurried downstairs as fast as she dared go.

He was sitting quite still in the golden glow of the sunset, staring out over the Grand Canal, Cas and Poll in his lap. He glanced up, but stayed where he was, his dark face unreadable.

The cats jumped down and padded to meet her. Luce stooped to greet both of them, then, crossing the room, she went down on her knees by his chair, and, taking his hand, held it against her cheek.

'I'm sorry,' she whispered. 'Oh, Michele, I'm sorry.'

He reversed the positions and, carrying her hand to his mouth, pressed a kiss into the palm. 'There's nothing to be sorry for.'

Almost dizzy with relief, she smiled brilliantly at him. 'I wanted to show you these.' She gave him the diaries. 'Please read them. I'm sure Mamma wouldn't mind.'

He scanned them in silence. Seated on the settee, she watched his face and realised that he was as moved as she had been. When he came to the part about the clip he glanced up, and she saw the flare of excitement in his silvery-green eyes before they dropped once again to the page.

After he'd finished reading he closed the last one almost reverently, and handed them back to her. 'Thank you, *cara*. I never knew where the second half of the clasp had gone. Do you know if she kept it?'

'I know she treasured it, though she never gave an inkling as to where it came from.' Luce felt in her pocket and passed it to him. She heard the indrawn breath hiss sharply through his teeth, and felt the wave of emotion that washed over him.

Paul had been quite wrong to call Michele cold and unfeeling. He was anything but.

Rising to his feet, he touched the light switch, dispelling the gathering gloom, before striding through to his office. He was only gone a moment or two and when he returned he was holding the complete clasp.

'A gold lion and a white unicorn against a blue shield was the first Michele's coat of arms,' he told her softly, resuming his seat. 'The lion signified the power and strength that were his, the unicorn, he wrote, symbolised the happiness Lucia brought to his house.

'This slightly altered and unique version, showing twin lions and a unicorn with a golden arrow in place of a horn, he had specially made.

'When they married, the two halves were joined, strength and happiness united by a crown. Ever since then the custom has been kept up and the two halves clasped together for the marriages where it is applicable.'

Before she could puzzle over his rather cryptic last sentence he continued, 'I don't know whether you noticed, but the doge was wearing it in the second of his portraits.'

'When I first saw the portrait, though the clasp didn't *consciously* register, my *subconscious* must have picked it up, because something I couldn't pin down nagged at me, and made me want to look again.'

'And did you?'

'Yes, I did. The second time I realised what it was. I didn't say anything to you because I needed time to think. But so much happened, and it had slipped my mind until I realised your father and my mother must have known each other in the past. That set me wondering, but it was reading the diary that made me know.'

After a moment she added thoughtfully, 'Have you any idea why your father didn't give it to your mother?'

'Because it wouldn't have been apt.'

Luce was about to ask him what he meant, when she

recalled him saying his father's marriage had been arranged, and hadn't proved a happy one, and bit her tongue.

At the same moment he queried, 'Have you read the latest diary?'

She shook her head. 'I. . .I wanted us both to read it at the same time.'

He patted his knee invitingly. Needing no further encouragement, Luce went and made herself comfortable, nestling against him.

This one was in English. Turning the pages together, they read what Luce Weston had written, getting a clear picture of someone who had loved more than she'd hated, and given more than she'd taken. A woman who had liked and respected her husband, and dearly loved her daughter. A woman who had made the most of what she'd got, and done her best to be content.

Then came September, and the words held a new and growing excitement.

It seems strange to think I'm going back home after all this time. Now at last I can admit to myself how much I've missed the sun and the warmth and the colour of Italy. . .

Is it possible to have a second chance of happiness? I hardly dare believe it. Ours was an unexpected meeting. Lorenzo and I looked at each other and nothing had changed. It was as if the intervening years had never been. . .

He wants me to marry him; he's as impetuous as a boy, and I feel seventeen again. . .

Tonight Lorenzo gave me the doge's ring, and told me the history of this lovely old house. He showed me the zodiac panelling, and Lucia's secret hiding-place.

It's time to go back to England and break the news

to Luce and Maureen. They are the only two I really care about. Please God I can make them understand how much this means to me. . .

Neither Lorenzo nor I want to part, but we'll be together again soon, and for always. . . I'm worried about wearing such a priceless ring. I've begged him to keep it until I get back, but he won't hear of it. . .

He'll be up in a moment. Our last night together; I leave first thing in the morning. Before I go I shall put the ring in a safe place, an appropriate place. I can't bring myself to take it. I have the strangest premonition. . .

The rest of the pages were blank.

Luce buried her face against Michele's neck and for a long time they sat without moving or speaking.

Eventually she stirred and found her voice. 'I wonder what Mamma meant by an appropriate place?'

'Your guess is as good as mine,' he admitted. 'But it seems certain that the answer lies in the old house.'

'Shall we go over there?' Luce asked breathlessly. 'Now?'

She nodded, and slipped off his knee.

Smiling at her eagerness, he unfastened the clasp and held out her half.

Jerkily she said, 'You keep it. I think it should stay together.'

He shook his head. 'Not yet, Luce. You can give it to me when the time is right.'

It was late when they arrived at the old house and by tacit consent they went straight to bed. Their feelings were intense, and he made love to her with an ardour she met and matched with a fiery passion that consumed them both in a blaze of glory.

Afterwards, when he drew her close, she went to sleep almost before she'd had time to savour the pleasure of lying in his arms.

176 JOY BRINGER

She slept long and dreamlessly and opened her eyes to a warm, sunny day. The space beside her was empty, and she felt a keen sense of loss that was instantly alleviated when the door opened and Michele came in, carrying a breakfast-tray.

He bent to kiss her lightly but lingeringly on the lips. '*Buon giorno, cara.* I don't need to ask if you slept well.'

When she just lay there, gazing up at him, glowing with happiness, he asked, 'Are you going to eat, or shall I join you?'

The gleam in his eyes left no doubt as to which he preferred.

She pushed herself up on one elbow and said impishly, 'The bread smells wonderful.'

He sighed. 'That serves me right for going out to fetch it fresh.'

'Not to mention the fruit and coffee.'

'What can you do with a woman who always thinks of her stomach first?'

'I suppose Didi doesn't?' Damn, damn, damn! What on earth had made her bring the American's name up?

Calmly he said, 'Didi doesn't eat breakfast.'

'I suppose you should know.' She must stop this, Luce told herself frantically. Why spoil what time they had together by sniping?

Looking not at all disturbed, he settled the tray across her knees and sat on the edge of the bed to pour coffee for them both.

Still a bit shy, Luce hitched the thin sheet a shade higher to cover her nakedness and, having trapped it under her arms, helped herself to a flaky roll, which she spread liberally with butter and apricot jam.

Michele sipped his black coffee and studied her. Made awkward by his amused scrutiny, she tilted the roll too much and a blob of jam dropped on to her chest between her breasts.

JOY BRINGER

He leaned forward and used the tip of his tongue to lick it off. Watching her nipples firm beneath the taut cotton, he smiled and, finding a sweet delight in teasing her, remarked, 'I'm pleased your excellent appetite extends to things other than food.'

Blushing rosily, unable to look at him, Luce concentrated on her breakfast. When she'd regained some degree of composure, she asked, 'Have you had any further thoughts as to where Mamma's "appropriate" place might be?'

'Earlier she'd mentioned the zodiac panelling and Lucia's secret hiding-place. . .'

'Of course,' Luce breathed.

'. . .unfortunately,' Michele went on, 'I haven't a clue as to where Lucia's secret hiding-place might be, so it comes down to a straightforward search.'

After breakfast and a quick shower they set about looking. Luce could barely contain her excitement, but after tapping and examining every inch of the panelling they were forced to admit defeat.

It must be easily accessible if you know where to look,' Michele remarked. 'But, for someone who *doesn't* know, in an old house like this it could take us months to find it.'

Luce pushed back her long dark hair, leaving a smudge of dust across her cheek. 'I take it Maria's been the housekeeper here for years. . . Is there any chance of *her* knowing?'

He took an immaculate hankie from his pocket and wiped the streak of dust from Luce's face, before answering, 'It's certainly worth a try.'

A phone call to Maria bore no fruit. Though she could well believe a secret hiding-place existed, the housekeeper said, she'd never stumbled on one, nor had Signor Diomede ever mentioned it.

Michele thanked her and rang off.

Luce chewed her underlip and stared into space.

178　　JOY BRINGER

Running a hand across the back of his neck, he asked, 'Have you an idea?'

'I keep thinking about the bed. I wonder if. . .'

'If what?'

She had just started to reply when the phone rang, cutting through her words.

He picked up the receiver. '*Sì*?' Leaning back, he crossed his legs. 'Ah, Didi. Did you have a good flight to London? Well, at least it's shorter than the one to New York. Yes, I hope so. . .'

Chilled and depressed, unwilling to sit there and listen to the conversation, Luce got to her feet and left, closing the door behind her.

She went up to the bedroom and gazed at the old four-poster, hardly noticing the faded splendour of its blue and gold canopy as she scrutinised the decorated wooden frieze that ran along the top.

Yes, there it was at the centre, just as she'd half recalled, a small panel carved with two stars and a Centaur aiming an arrow into the night sky. The half-man, half-horse archer, symbol of Sagittarius, would certainly be appropriate, Luce thought.

A heavy oak chair stood by the window. Having dragged it over, she stood on it with care, and found it brought her eyes level with the frieze.

Crooking a finger, she tapped experimentally, and caught her breath. Apart from a bit of woodworm, the beam seemed solid enough, but the panel rang hollow.

A delicate and painstaking examination with her fingertips yielded nothing. Next she pressed each of the raised portions on the carving, but without success.

She was wondering what else to try when her finger-nail slid into a tiny groove on the inside edge of the uppermost star. Almost immediately her thumbnail found another groove opposite; she *pulled*, and the star came out about a centimetre.

When nothing else happened disappointment diluted

JOY BRINGER

179

her excitement. But she'd found the answer to part of the puzzle, so surely it should be possible to solve it completely?

Not another thing would pull, and she'd already tried pressing everything. . . But suppose there was something that could only be depressed after the first piece had been pulled into the right position?

The instant she touched it Luce felt the second star dip beneath the pressure of her finger. She gave a little crow of triumph when suddenly there was a sharp click, and the panel opened like a tiny door.

Deep inside the cavity was a small, dark chamois bag with a draw-string neck.

Feeling it should be Michele who recovered it, Luce drew a long, steadying breath and turned to climb down.

A strong hand closed around her arm, making her jump. She'd been so engrossed that she hadn't heard him come in.

Frowning a little, he helped her to descend. 'Standing on chairs isn't to be recommended when you're just recovering from a sprained ankle. Why didn't you wait for me?'

'I should have thought that was obvious,' she said flatly.

He glanced from her empty hands up to the panel.

'You seem to have discovered Lucia's secret hiding-place. It's a great pity it's not the right one.' With a sigh he admitted, 'I *was* hoping to find the ring quickly.'

'So you can give it to your wife-to-be before she gets too impatient?'

Smiling at her, he agreed, 'Something like that.'

Her voice brittle, Luce suggested, 'Well, you'd better phone her back and tell her it's been found.'

For what seemed an age he stood stock-still, his silvery-green eyes on her face, then he reached up and, feeling in the cavity, retrieved its contents. Having

180 .JOY BRINGER

weighed the bag in his hand, he slipped it into his pocket.

The next instant Luce was seized and whirled around joyously before being swung up into his arms. He descended the stairs two at a time, and before she'd managed to catch her breath she was deposited on the settee in the living-room and Michele was sitting beside her.

He took out the bag, undid the strings, and tipped the ring into his palm.

Luce gasped as the huge ruby glowed as red as blood. No wonder Didi couldn't wait to wear it; it was truly magnificent. But, as far as *she* was concerned, it brought only sadness in its wake, precipitating, as it no doubt would, Michele's marriage to the American.

'My clever girl!' he was saying exultantly. 'Having found the panel, how did you discover the trick to opening it?'

She told him.

'What inspired you to try the bed?' he wanted to know.

'I'd half noticed the Centaur carving, and "an appropriate place" suddenly struck a chord.'

'Well, it was certainly that.'

Luce frowned. 'Was Lucia a Sagittarian?'

'Yes, she was, though I wasn't thinking of Lucia.'

'But you couldn't have known Mamma was a Sagittarian.'

'Yes, I knew. So how many days were there between you two?'

'I was born on November the twenty-seventh, her birthday.'

'A lovely present.' He cupped Luce's cheek with his palm and smiled into her eyes, making her heart do what felt like a series of back somersaults. Then, his expression suddenly turning serious, he said, 'I owe you an abject apology.'

She shook her head. 'I don't blame you, really. The whole thing has been so strange.'

He nodded. 'Fate works in mysterious ways.'

'That's what Aunt Maureen said.'

'Speaking of Aunt Maureen, don't you think we should give her the good news?'

'Yes, I suppose we should.' Luce dialled the number of the gallery, remarking, 'She'll be at work, but Liz should be able to hold the fort it necessary.'

Maureen answered straight away, and listened eagerly, giving excited squeaks from time to time as her niece brought her up to date on everything that had happened.

'So all's well that ends well, to quote Shakespeare,' she said cheerfully when Luce had finished. 'What will you be doing now?' Without pause, she answered her own question. 'I suppose staying on to finish organising the exhibition, among other things.'

She sighed happily, then went on, 'We seem to have a prospective buyer and Liz is making frantic signals to me, so I'd better go. Don't forget to let your old auntie know how the *other things* are progressing, but I'm sure everything will work out just fine.'

Luce replaced the receiver and sighed in her turn. If only everything would. But of course it wasn't that simple. Maureen didn't know anywhere near the whole story. . .

She didn't know the promised "exhibition" had been only a trick to get her niece to come to Venice, or that Michele Diomede was also Peter Sebastian, and she didn't known about Didi Lombard. But she *did* know that Michele was a Gemini, which made her patent enthusiasm seem peculiar to say the least. . .

'Twenty lire for your thoughts,' Michele offered, adding, with a smile that tugged at her heart-strings, 'Of course, that's not my final bid; I may be willing to go a little higher if they're worth it.'

JOY BRINGER

Luce shook her head. 'I hardly think they're worth bankrupting yourself for.'

'Then will you settle for a kiss?'

A kiss before parting, she thought, and lifted her face, her golden-brown eyes suddenly sparkling with tears. Her mother had lived her life as fully as possible without the man she loved; *she* could do the same.

When his lips touched hers the tears overflowed. He kissed them away while Luce silently struggled for self-control.

Letting her go, he sat back and studied her, his black head tilted a little to one side. 'Well?'

When she just gazed at him, he said patiently, 'I've paid the agreed price, so tell me why, when you ought to be jubilant, you're so obviously sad.'

'I was wondering about. . .about going home. How soon will you be leaving Venice?'

'That depends on the woman in my life.'

She'd known he would follow Didi as soon as the ring was found and the American wanted him by her side, but still his words brought such pain that for a moment Luce thought she'd moaned aloud.

He lifted her left hand, playing with it, separating the fingers and planting baby kisses on each one. Then before she realised his intention he had slipped the doge's ring on to her third finger. Though the stone was large, the ornate gold band was small, and it fitted as if it had been made for her.

The huge ruby looked wonderful on her slim, but capable hand and she gazed at it as though mesmerised.

'Come upstairs with me,' he invited softly. 'I can't wait to make love to you while you're wearing nothing but that.'

With a strangled gasp of fury she tried to pull it off, but he held both her hands, preventing her.

'If you think for one moment I'm going to wear

another woman's ring while you make love to me you've got another think coming. . .' she choked.

He raised a black, winged brow. 'I'm sure Lucia wouldn't mind. You have a lot in common. Both your names mean light, both of you have——'

'What about Didi?' she broke in. 'I'm sure *she'd* mind. And we've *nothing* in common.' Except that we love the same man, she added silently.

But *did* Didi love him, or was it his wealth, his position in life, his *talent* that she cared about?

With a wry little twist to his lips Michele observed, 'I'm rather pleased that you two have nothing in common. . . I thought at one time Didi and I would get along well enough, but, after finding my sweet, simple, clumsy, courageous, honest, fiery. . .' his voice dropped to a husky whisper '. . .*beautiful, passionate* Sagittarian, I know no other woman would have satisfied me.'

'You mean. . .?' She gaped at him.

'Your mouth's open, and it's giving me ideas. . .'

Refusing to be side-tracked, she threatened shakily, 'Tell me what you mean, or I'll thump you.'

'I mean, whether you wear the ring or not has nothing whatever to do with Didi. Before I put her on the plane for London I told her everything was over between us and I've just reiterated that.

'I mean, I love you to distraction and want to marry you. I need you to love me and make me whole, to live with me for the rest of our lives and be the pride of my heart and the mother of my children. . .'

Nonchalantly she said, 'Oh, well, if *that's* all. . .'

'So come to bed.'

Needing no further urging, she threw herself into his arms and he carried her upstairs. Swiftly and efficiently he took off her clothes and his own. Then he laid her on the bed and feasted his eyes on her, slender and seductive, totally naked except for the glowing ruby that flashed fire whenever she moved her hand.

Flushed and radiant, she smiled up at him and held out her arms, welcoming him as Lucia must have welcomed her Michele.

It was much later when, as she lay contentedly against his heart, a dark cloud suddenly appeared on her golden horizon.

Although she hadn't said a word, he lifted his black head and, peering into her face, asked, 'What is it?'

She sat up.

He followed suit, and, leaning back against the pillows, put a comforting arm around her. 'What's wrong, *cara*?'

'Nothing's wrong.' She stared down at her hands. 'It's just that. . . Do you really believe star signs make any difference?'

'A great deal of difference.'

'Oh,' she whispered forlornly. 'Then perhaps I shouldn't marry you, after all. When we first talked about our star signs I said they made us——'

'Incompatible,' he finished for her. 'And you were quite wrong.'

'But we're complete opposites.'

He laughed. 'My darling idiot, I know that. But opposites attract, especially when they're the opposite sex. We each have the qualities the other needs. Together we make a perfect whole.

'You're fire and I'm air. No fire can burn without the oxygen air provides, and air can only rise to great heights when it's warmed by fire.

'When they're right for each other a Gemini and a Sagittarian can have a wonderful, magical, *lasting* relationship. Take the Lion of Venice and his Lucia. . .'

'You mean *they* were. . .?'

'Didn't the carving on the panel tell you? Castor and

JOY BRINGER

Pollux, twin stars in the constellation of Gemini, and the Sagittarian Centaur.

'And that's not all. My father was a Gemini, and I knew your mother was a Sagittarian as soon as I found he'd given her half the clip. I told you the first Michele had it specially made. The two lions, as well as standing for strength and power, signified the Gemini twins, while the unicorn with a golden arrow for a horn symbolised the Sagittarian archer and happiness.'

'I see,' Luce said slowly. 'So the clip was only appropriate when both star signs matched.'

'Exactly. And if you delve into the family archives you'll find that over the centuries, on the somewhat rare occasions when the two halves have been clasped together, the marriages are recorded as being extremely happy ones.'

She rubbed her cheek against his chest and breathed in the clean male scent of him. 'I see now why you said I could give it back to you when the time was right.'

His arm tightened around her. 'So how soon will you marry me?'

'As soon as you like,' she said, feeling almost light-headed with happiness. 'You don't mind if I invite Aunt Maureen?'

'Of course not. Do you think she'll be pleased?'

'I'm sure she will.'

'You haven't asked her which star sign was right for you?'

'I don't need to. It occurred to me that she knew you were a Gemini, and she was clearly thrilled about us getting together.'

He grinned. 'I'm rather thrilled myself. What about you?'

By way of answering, she threw her arms around his neck and hugged him tightly.

'You're strangling me,' he said mildly. 'But I like it, so don't stop, my little joy bringer.'

STARGAZING

YOUR STAR SIGN: **SAGITTARIUS (November 23rd–December 22nd)**

SAGITTARIUS is the third of the Fire signs, which makes you enthusiastic, energetic and opinionated. You are adventurous and love to travel, becoming very restless if you have to stay in one place for too long. Boredom is your greatest enemy! Sagittarians are natural optimists, with a great zest for life and an eager curiosity, loving to learn new things. Your wit and gregarious nature make you the life and soul of the party, but your desire for honesty can make you seem blunt and tactless. Your many friends also have to tolerate the way you moralise, without ever 'practising what you preach'. Sagittarians aren't very domesticated and so, while you are off pursuing your many interests and entertaining others, your long-suffering family are probably doing your housework and paying the bills!

Your characteristics in love: Sagittarius is the hunter of the Zodiac; enjoying the chase but perhaps losing interest once the prey is in your grasp. You may well value companionship above passion but you would probably prefer a series of flirtations to long-term relationships. You value time on your own and your independence is very important to you. All of this can be rather hard on the partners of Sagittarians, but once you are involved in a relationship you are warm and caring, and great fun to be with.

Star signs which are compatible with you: Aries, **Leo**, **Libra** and **Aquarius** are the most harmonious, while **Gemini**, **Pisces** and **Virgo** will be a challenge. Partners born under other signs can be compatible, depending on which planets reside in their houses of Personality and Romance.

What is your star-career? Restless Sagittarians would probably place job satisfaction higher than financial rewards on their list of priorities when choosing a career. You don't like rigid planning and structures and you are more of an 'ideas' person, with your initiative and inspiration proving very valuable to your company. And you would always rather leave it to someone else to carry out the boring legwork! Your thirst for knowledge and sense of fun make jobs in teaching and performing attractive to Sagittarians. Careers in travel, law, writing, sport, the military and sales may also appeal.

Your colours and birthstones: Being a Fire sign, Sagittarians love the warm shades of reds, purples and browns.

Your birthstone, the turquoise, has always been said to protect the wearer against dark forces, and is worn by lovers as a sign of fidelity: it might remind roving Sagittarians not to stray!

SAGITTARIUS ASTRO-FACTFILE

Day of the week: Thursday.
Countries: Spain, Hungary, Australia, U.S.A.
Flowers: Narcissus, dandelion, pinks.
Food: Blueberries and asparagus. Sagittarians are not especially interested in food, except as a means of fuelling their energy levels, and prefer traditional meals like stew or Ploughman's lunch. You particularly enjoy picnics and cooking over a real campfire.
Health: Sagittarians are often sporty types, but do tend towards laziness and to indulging in bouts of eating and drinking. You are particularly prone to liver, hip and thigh problems. Try different forms of relaxation techniques to counter-balance your restlessness.

You share your star sign with these famous names:

Woody Allen	Jane Fonda
Steven Spielberg	Judi Dench
Kirk Douglas	Bette Midler
Frank Sinatra	Pamela Stevenson
Ian Botham	Chris Evert

Four brand new romances from favourite Mills & Boon authors have been specially selected to make your Christmas special.

THE FINAL SURRENDER
Elizabeth Oldfield

SOMETHING IN RETURN
Karen van der Zee

HABIT OF COMMAND
Sophie Weston

CHARADE OF THE HEART
Cathy Williams

Published in November 1992   Price: £6.80

Available from Boots, Martins, John Menzies, W.H. Smith, most supermarkets and other paperback stockists. Also available from Mills & Boon Reader Service, PO Box 236, Thornton Road, Croydon, Surrey CR9 3RU.

BARBARY WHARF

Will Gina Tyrrell succeed in her plans to oust
Nick Caspian from the Sentinel –
or will Nick fight back?

There is only one way for Nick to win, but it might,
in the end, cost him everything!

The final book in the Barbary Wharf series

SURRENDER

Available from November 1992   Price: £2.99

W●RLDWIDE

*Available from Boots, Martins, John Menzies, W.H. Smith,
most supermarkets and other paperback stockists.
Also available from Mills & Boon Reader Service, PO Box 236,
Thornton Road, Croydon, Surrey CR9 3RU.*

Accept 4 FREE Romances and 2 FREE gifts

FROM READER SERVICE

An irresistible invitation from Mills & Boon Reader Service. Please accept our offer of 4 free Romances, a CUDDLY TEDDY and a special MYSTERY GIFT... Then, if you choose, go on to enjoy 6 captivating Romances every month for just £1.70 each, postage and packing free. Plus our FREE Newsletter with author news, competitions and much more.

**Send the coupon below to:
Reader Service, FREEPOST,
PO Box 236, Croydon,
Surrey CR9 9EL.**

NO STAMP REQUIRED

Yes! Please rush me 4 Free Romances and 2 free gifts!
Please also reserve me a Reader Service Subscription. If I decide to subscribe I can look forward to receiving 6 brand new Romances each month for just £10.20, post and packing free.
If I choose not to subscribe I shall write to you within 10 days - I can keep the books and gifts whatever I decide. I may cancel or suspend my subscription at any time. I am over 18 years of age.

Ms/Mrs/Miss/Mr _____ EP30R

Address _____

_____

Postcode_____ Signature _____

Offer expires 31st May 1993. The right is reserved to refuse an application and change the terms of this offer. Readers overseas and in Eire please send for details.
Southern Africa write to Book Services International Ltd, P.O. Box 42654, Craighall, Transvaal 2024.
You may be mailed with offers from other reputable companies as a result of this application. If you would prefer not to share in this opportunity, please tick box ☐

Next Month's Romances

Each month you can choose from a wide variety of romance with Mills & Boon. Below are the new titles to look out for next month, why not ask either Mills & Boon Reader Service or your Newsagent to reserve you a copy of the titles you want to buy — just tick the titles you would like and either post to Reader Service or take it to any Newsagent and ask them to order your books.

Please save me the following titles:	Please tick	√
BACHELOR AT HEART	Roberta Leigh	
TIDEWATER SEDUCTION	Anne Mather	
SECRET ADMIRER	Susan Napier	
THE QUIET PROFESSOR	Betty Neels	
ONE-NIGHT STAND	Sandra Field	
THE BRUGES ENGAGEMENT	Madeleine Ker	
AND THEN CAME MORNING	Daphne Clair	
AFTER ALL THIS TIME	Vanessa Grant	
CONFRONTATION	Sarah Holland	
DANGEROUS INHERITANCE	Stephanie Howard	
A MAN FOR CHRISTMAS	Annabel Murray	
DESTINED TO LOVE	Jennifer Taylor	
AN IMAGE OF YOU	Liz Fielding	
TIDES OF PASSION	Sally Heywood	
DEVIL'S DREAM	Nicola West	
HERE COMES TROUBLE	Debbie Macomber	

If you would like to order these books in addition to your regular subscription from Mills & Boon Reader Service please send £1.70 per title to: Mills & Boon Reader Service, P.O. Box 236, Croydon, Surrey, CR9 3RU, quote your Subscriber No:..
(If applicable) and complete the name and address details below. Alternatively, these books are available from many local Newsagents including W.H.Smith, J.Menzies, Martins and other paperback stockists from 4th December 1992.

Name:..

Address:...

....Post Code:..........................

To Retailer: If you would like to stock M&B books please contact your regular book/magazine wholesaler for details.

You may be mailed with offers from other reputable companies as a result of this application. If you would rather not take advantage of these opportunities please tick box ☐